The Pierhead Jum

Ronald Bassett joined the
cruiser *Norfolk* in which he
during the *Bismarck* action, and the North African landings. He served in landing craft during the invasion of Normandy.

Also by
Ronald Basset in Pan Books

The Tinfish Run

Ronald Basset

The Pierhead Jump

Pan Books in association with
Macmillan London

First published 1978 by Macmillan London Ltd
This edition published 1979 by Pan Books Ltd,
Cavaye Place, London SW10 9PG
in association with Macmillan London Ltd

ISBN 0 330 25833 8
Printed and bound in Great Britain by
Richard Clay (The Chaucer Press) Ltd, Bungay, Suffolk

For a glossary of naval lower-deck terminology and technical terms see the end of the book (p. 148)

author's foreword

Signalman Lobby Ludd, whom we have already met aboard HMS *Virtue* in *The Tinfish Run*, is a fictitious character whose experiences, however, will be not unfamiliar to thousands of men who served in the Royal Navy during the war of 1939–45. His new ship, the cruiser *Daemon*, is also a fictitious vessel, as are all others involved in *The Pierhead Jump*, but it is almost impossible to select a plausible name that has not been owned by some warship at some time. Any similarities to real vessels, or to real persons, past or present, are entirely coincidental.

The narrative was suggested by an actual series of events that followed the torpedoing of the White Star liner *Laconia* by U-156 in September 1942. The factual circumstances, however, are only very loosely followed, and the relationship is mentioned only to indicate that the story is far from incredible.

one

By late 1942, HMS *Drake*, otherwise Royal Naval Barracks, Keyham, Devonport, was an immense, sprawling complexity of slum buildings enclosed by high walls and teeming with shipless naval ratings of every branch, background and philosophy, but all sharing one common sentiment – a detestation of their environment and a fervent desire to be free of it at the earliest opportunity.

One of three similar port division depots – the others were in Portsmouth and Chatham – RNB Devonport had been built to accommodate the temporarily uncommitted men of a peacetime navy and was totally inadequate for the massive expansion in personnel that the war had introduced. During those peacetime years of governmental cheese-paring, when every available penny had to be spent in providing the Navy's ships with an outward appearance of efficiency, the barracks had been allowed to fall to a level of dilapidation that no amount of hasty renovation could improve. Complete demolition and rebuilding were impossible; any accommodation was better than none, and the ugly, outmoded buildings that had crumbled to squalidness for years remained in that condition. There was only one thing that could be done about RNB – get out of it as soon as possible.

However, getting in initially was a frustrating procedure. Most incoming ratings had been drafted from docked ships for a number of reasons, either singly or in groups of up to several hundred, and wished only to proceed on leave or be drafted to another ship, but 'joining routine' must first be suffered. There was a warren of dingy administrative offices – the Regulating Office, Pay Office, Duty Watch Office, Victualling Office, Drafting Office – and at the small window of each the new arrivals queued to have their credentials scrutinized and their immediate disposal determined. Their kits must be inspected and deficiencies made good, overdue vaccinations and inoculations sought from the Sick Bay. Nothing could be achieved, no future was apparent, until this joining routine was satisfactorily completed, and it might go on for several days. If, at the end of it, there was no leave to claim or no ship to join, they must be swallowed among the thousands who wandered aimlessly, slung their hammocks nightly in noisy barrack-rooms crowded to suffocation, in basements, the gymnasium, in damp Nissen huts around the playing-fields, or anywhere. They ate in Jago's, the vast, dreary mess-hall whose greasy tables could accommodate the barracks' population only in several sittings, or went to an equally crowded and dreary NAAFI for a Cornish pasty among tea-sloppings and tobacco-smoke. As days stretched into weeks, despair deepened. There were stories of men disappearing into the congested ant-heap of RNB never to be seen again, to be forgotten for the war's duration, and nobody doubted it. If there had ever been any pattern, any logical method in the barracks' daily programme, it had long been overwhelmed by sheer weight of numbers. Useless employment for the sake of employment was imposed by masters-at-arms, regulating petty officers and gunners' mates who could have offered no explanation other than that it was orders. No officer ever trod among the crowded, jostling cattle of RNB; it might have been unwise for him to do so.

Provost patrols, distinguished by belts, gaiters, armlets and swinging batons, prowled the barracks and its environs – the beer canteen, the cinema, the main gate, vehicle-park, mess-hall, gunnery school and jetty. Duty watchmen and defaulters mustered in the dusty drill shed eyed wistfully the masts of ships in the nearby Tamar.

There was a small, privileged few who did not share the majority's loathing for RNB. They included those men who were natives of the Devonport locality, who could sleep in their own beds three nights out of four and be paid a lodging allowance for doing so. They placed their domestic interests first, and had little sympathy for the discomforts of the many. It was from these that a large percentage of the barracks' administrative personnel was drawn. There was also a handful of middle-aged reservists, recalled to the service after years of civilian life, who had decided that even RNB could not be worse than a destroyer in the Arctic, and had contrived to achieve employment in office or dockyard, taking comfort in the thought that the war could not last for ever.

Finally, as in any large, closely herded community, there was the criminal element, for which RNB was a kind of heaven; there were thousands of kitbags, untended clothing, suitcases, personal valuables and money. Thieves moved through the barrack-rooms and baggage-stores of RNB with the voracity of locusts, and an unsuspecting newcomer, within hours, could find himself with no other possessions than the clothes he wore. Authority shrugged, indifferent. The problem of theft was too big, victims had only themselves to blame and, anyway, authority had a bus to catch at 16.30.

Local economy was firmly geared to the Royal Naval Dockyard, to which RNB was a necessary partner, tolerated as such. There had never been any fraternal relationships between naval personnel and dockyard employees, and in wartime, when almost every second or third person in Plymouth and Devonport was a bluejacket, there were no patriotic illusions. When a war-battered heavy cruiser limped into dock for repairs, local voices were raised in protest. Such a ship would only invite enemy air attacks. There were limits to loyalty. Take the ship somewhere else – anywhere else, but not here.

Devonport offered little comfort to the shore-going rating except shabby pubs or the bleak austerity of temperance hostels – the Seamen's Rest, the Salvation Army, the Mission to Seamen – which had hardly changed in character since their controversial introduction by Miss Agnes Weston in 1876. For the man who looked for something other than pints of ale and blowsy tarts, or mugs of stewed tea and Bible texts, there was neighbouring Plymouth, with more pubs and tarts, fish-and-chip shops, tattooists and photographers, naval tailors, out-of-bounds hotels and local indifference. The belated, war-inspired provision of a NAAFI Club with carpeted floors, easy chairs and potted shrubs did nothing to relieve the rating's unremitting loneliness and homesickness. He yearned for simple things – a domestic environment, his own small bedroom, ablutions in private, freedom from coarseness and bullying superiors – but he would find none of these things in a naval port. He had been incensed by the suggestion of Lady Astor, Member of

Parliament for the area, that all men returning from a foreign station should be compelled to wear a yellow armlet to indicate that they might have VD.

Signalman Charlie Ludd, D/JX245613, Church of England, Ship's Book Number 4602, badges nil, tattoos nil, mole on left shoulder and appendix scar, eyes grey, hair brown, complexion fresh, no criminal record, conduct assessment VG, lowered his kitbag wearily to the ground and offered his station card to the frowning face beyond the window-hatch of the Drafting Office. 'Ludd,' he said, and waited.

'Ludd,' the Regulating Petty Officer grunted. 'We've been piping for you all bleedin' forenoon. You got cloth ears? Where've yer been?'

'Queueing fer jabs in the Sick Bay,' the other explained. 'I've got more 'oles in me than a soddin' NAAFI sponge-cake—'

The RPO bridled. 'You get stroppy with me, lad,' he threatened, 'and I'll get stroppy with you – see? If you 'adn't got a pierhead jump, you'd be up the quarterdeck with yer cap off, smartish.' He groped for a sheaf of papers. 'Ludd, ex-*Virtue*, right? – and just back off survivor's and sick leave.' He sniffed. 'While you've been arsing around on leave there's been a war on, in case you ain't 'eard.'

'Yes,' Ludd said flatly. 'There was a buzz going round, but I didn't know fer sure.'

Lobby Ludd – he would not have turned his head if anyone had shouted the name he had been baptized with – was suffering the desponding withdrawal symptoms common to all sailors returning from home leave to the purgatory of RNB. It was criminally unjust that, at nineteen, life should offer no prospect other than carrying a heavy kitbag from one dreary location to another because he dare not lose sight of it for a single moment, getting a station card rubber-stamped in a dozen obscure and widely separated venues for no apparent reason, and being snarled at for his inability to be in two places at the same time.

'Get your bag and 'ammock into the fourteen-thirty dockyard truck, Ludd, and don't be adrift. You're joinin' *Daemon*, lying at number four berth. She's got sailin' orders for sixteen hundred, and if you ain't aboard the Commodore will be requestin' the pleasure o' your company—'

'*Daemon?* Shave off.' Lobby Ludd sucked his teeth. 'I'm bleedin' Second o' Port – duty watch last night and a soddin' draft chit today. Don't I get time ter write a bleedin' letter? And what's *Daemon*?'

'Never mind *what* it is, Ludd,' the RPO advised. 'Just get *on* it, that's all. And you can write a letter from Gib.'

'One day,' Lobby Ludd told the clock over the distant quarterdeck, 'when we 'ave the Revolution, we're going ter 'ang all bleedin' crushers on meat 'ooks—'

The RPO jerked upright. 'What was that, Ludd?'

'I said, if I'd known, I'd have 'ad my soddin' 'air cut.' He lifted his kitbag to his shoulder.

The driver of the 14.30 dockyard truck was a greying, three-badge able seaman with a paunch and a nicotine-stained upper lip. '*Daemon*? Yer ain't never got a draft chit ter *Daemon*, Bunts?' He shook his head. 'Yer poor bastard. Can't yer go sick? Tell 'em yer've got a weak bladder. Better still' – he glanced around – 'if yer like, I'll run the truck over yer foot, accidental—'

Lobby Ludd considered. 'Why? What's wrong wi' *Daemon* – apart from the usual?' He was reluctant to show his ignorance by asking what type of ship *Daemon* was. 'She floats, don't she?'

'She's a bleedin' Jonah, mate. She always 'as been. I s'pose you're replacing the bloke that drank lysol last week.'

'Lysol?'

'Bunting-tosser – drank a pint o' lysol in his 'ammock. It didn't do 'im much good, but it got 'im ashore. Feet first.'

Lobby Ludd was mildly startled. 'Shave off.' He frowned. 'What d'yer mean, she's a Jonah?'

The able seaman was delighted to be the harbinger of pessimistic information. 'It all started when she was launched – a dockyard matie was crushed. Then, in 'er first sub-calibre shoot, B-turret blew up an' killed four ratings. Since then she's stripped 'er turbines, 'ad two fires, wrapped 'er wire round 'er screws, and rammed a submarine in Liverpool Bay that was built fer the Argentine Navy. Then she ran aground off Calshot when the *Scharnhorst* an' *Gneisenau* got through the Channel, and 'er skipper was court-martialled.' He grinned, enjoying himself. 'She's the only ship in the dockyard what nobody's volunteered for. If yer like, I'll drop yer off at Albert Gate, and yer can 'ide in the railway tunnel till she's slipped. Yer can always say yer got lost.'

All things considered, Lobby Ludd decided, perhaps RNB Devonport wasn't so bad after all. Well, it could be worse. *Daemon*, for starters. No, sod it – this old three-badger was full of flannel. If *Daemon* had suffered a series of misfortunes, it didn't mean that her future would follow the same pattern. Besides, lightning didn't strike twice ...

He had been at the foot of the bridge-ladder when two torpedoes had struck the old destroyer almost simultaneously, and she had broken her back and sunk in minutes. It had seemed inhumanly unfair, after all that had happened before, that *Virtue* should be destroyed when only hours from a home port, only a few miles from the Scottish coast. They had survived an outward passage to Murmansk during which all other ships of the convoy's escort had been lost – a sister destroyer, a corvette and two armed trawlers – and there was not a man among them who was not thinking only of tomorrow's docking and ten day's leave, away from it all. But none of *Virtue*'s company had caught that train from Newcastle Central. Some of them died with the ship, others had fought for life in the cold, grey sea until exhaustion defeated them – like Bungy Williams and Stripey Albright – and something within him, too, had died that day. Later, in the warm below decks of the minesweeper from Aberdeen, he had wept with the agony of circulation returning to his frozen limbs. He had both legs broken, and did not care if he lived, until the prick of a needle brought blessed oblivion.

He had a confused recollection of a distant shrill of ambulance bells, the glare of lights, hospital smells, women's quiet voices, but most of all of luxurious warmth and a sense of wellbeing. It was a delightful limbo in which he would have been content to float for ever, but someone was chiding. 'Now, come along, Mr Ludd. You've slept for twenty hours, and it's time I gave you a bath and a shave.' She was petite and very pretty. His legs were long, white cocoons, the feet raised by pulleys, and he wore a garment that resembled a Victorian nightgown. She placed a basin at the bedside and rolled back her starched cuffs.

Lobby Ludd remembered everything. 'Shave?' he asked. 'Shave what?'

'Your face,' she said, not amused. 'And you're smothered with dirty oil, so we'll take your bed-shirt off—'

'Roll on,' he protested. 'I'll tell yer what. You do the top arf, see—'

'*Mister* Ludd,' she informed him firmly, 'I am not unacquainted with certain features of male anatomy, and I am sure that yours comply with the usual pattern. If you're embarrassed, shut your eyes.'

He shut his eyes. This was what Bungy Williams had told him about, in Polyarnoe – steam baths, and being massaged by naked women, then whipped with sticks. It was bleedin' marvellous, Bungy had promised. Well, Lobby conceded, it was very nice but, if a bloke wasn't accustomed to having his John Thomas washed with warm soap and water by a pretty little pusher, there was likely to be a disturbing consequence, and there was nothing he could do about it.

She sighed. 'That's very clever, Mr Ludd, and I'm very impressed. Now, what's your next trick?'

The truck drew into the jetty and halted. 'There she is, mate,' the AB said. '*Daemon*. All bull an' brightwork – everything in accordance wi' KRs an' AIs. Nobody takes any soddin' chances, jes' in case, and everyone's waiting for the next thing ter go wrong. If I was you, Bunts, I wouldn't touch *anything*, in case it comes off in yer bleedin' 'and.' He glanced at the sky. 'What did I tell yer? It's startin' ter rain.'

The light cruiser moored alongside was immaculate, her pale blue-and-white paintwork as fresh as if only hours old, her brass gleaming, steel burnished, and greyed decks spotless. Even the trickle of smoke that rose from each funnel seemed clean. Her boats were precisely stowed, and it was impossible to imagine that her well-scrubbed cables and anchors had ever lain in the mud of the sea bottom. By comparison with *Virtue*, in which every day was a battle against rust and soot, decks were worn to bare metal, and everything leaked brown water, *Daemon* was a thing of sterile perfection.

He had reported himself to the Officer of the Watch, recorded his arrival at the ship's Regulating Office, and had just reached 12-Mess, forward on the lower deck, when the SRE shrieked. *'Special sea dutymen close up. Secure all scuttles and watertight doors. Hands fall in for leaving harbour.'* In a messdeck empty of other occupants, Lobby Ludd continued to transfer the contents of his kitbag to a bulkhead locker. Everything smelled of fresh paint and yellow soap, the tables were whitely scoured, messtraps polished, hammocks neatly stowed in their netting. 'Shave off,' he sniffed, and unrolled his socks.

There was an angry bellow. 'And why aren't you fell in on the upper deck? Did you 'ear the pipe?' It was the Master-at-Arms, grim-faced. 'What's yer name?'

'Ludd – Signalman. As a matter of fact—'

'Don't give me lip. In this ship *everyone* falls in fer leaving an' entering 'arbour, including sparkers an' buntings, see. Ludd, eh? All right, I've got yer number. The next time, you're fer the 'igh jump, Ludd—'

The SRE shrieked again. *'Attention on the upper deck. Face to port.'*

Seven hours later, 150 miles due west of Ushant, and in bright moonlight, *Korvetten-Kapitän* Reinhard Behrmann swore softly on the bridge of U-157 as the distant but distinctly visible warship moved across his bows from left to right. He lowered his glasses and turned to his First Lieutenant. 'Light cruiser. Two funnels. C- or D-class. Course one-twenty-five, speed twenty-five knots. A pity, Jensen.'

It was a pity, but the British cruiser was just beyond the U-boat's grasp; even at his best surface speed of eighteen knots, Behrmann would not achieve an interception, and it would soon be dawn, when he must dive for safety from prowling Coastal Command aircraft. It was a pity. He watched until the enemy ship had disappeared to the south-west, then sighed.

'Clear the bridge. Take her down to thirty metres. Resume passage.'

Behrmann had brought the U-boat from the Baltic, where she had recently completed four months with the 4th Training Flotilla, passing through the Kiel Canal, northward to the Shetlands, through Rockall and down the west coast of Ireland. His destination was St-Nazaire, and the long, circuitous route, safer than that through the Channel, allowed more leisurely opportunities for working up a less-than-experienced crew and for ascertaining any defects in the submarine's performance. In consequence, Berhmann was not looking for trouble, but the enemy cruiser would have been a welcome kill to boost his crew's morale. It was a pity.

U-157 was a large, ocean-going submarine of the Type IX/C, of 1051 tons surfaced and 1232 tons submerged, carrying a crew of five officers and forty-six ratings. This class was of larger capacity and longer endurance than the commoner Type VII, but took longer to build and was usually deployed in more distant waters than the Western Approaches. U-157's endurance was sixty days, or 11,000 miles at 12 knots, having a maximum surface speed of 18 knots or 7 knots submerged; 240 feet long, she had 6 torpedo tubes – four bow and two stern – and stowed 22 torpedoes. She also mounted 88mm, 37mm and 20mm deck-guns.

Behrmann's hunting-ground was going to be the eastern seaboard of the United States, where there was little organized naval defence and the neon lights of coastal resorts could be seen twenty miles out at sea. First, however, his orders from *Befehlshaber der Unterseeboote* required him to reach the submarine pens of St-Nazaire without taking unnecessary risks, for refuelling, provisioning, and a final briefing. After that, U-157 would have more exciting quarry than the old Norwegian hulks used for torpedo training in the Baltic.

3,500 miles westward, it was only 17.30 hours Eastern Time as Montauk Point faded astern of the *Susquehanna* and the coastguard cutter turned away with a last whoop of her klaxon towards Long Island Sound. The big merchantman increased to twelve knots, then fifteen, thrusting aside the long Atlantic rollers with all the ease of her 19,000 tons. Nothing lay between her bows and the distant coasts of Africa and Spain.

Susquehanna, owned by the Eagle Steamship and Export Company and under charter to the United States Maritime Commission, had spent the previous fifteen years carrying passengers and mixed cargoes between New York, Charleston, Miami and New Orleans and fighting a losing battle against the growing competition from internal airlines. Now, however, an army of carpenters and welders had partitioned cabins, turned her holds into accommodation-decks lined with hundreds of bunks, installed additional kitchens, mess-spaces and latrines. *Susquehanna* was a war transport with a capacity for 4,000, oil-fired turbine engines, twin screws and a useful top speed of twenty knots. It was this last factor that had persuaded the Navy Department not to confine her to a nine-knot convoy but to allow her to proceed unescorted.

To the casual observer there was nothing unusual about *Susquehanna*, but below decks she was no ordinary troopship. Accommodation areas were enclosed within steel mesh, all deadlights and many doors had been welded shut, and there were walkways for sentries. Notices and warnings were painted in German and Italian in addition to English.

It was March 1943, and the Anglo-American campaign in North Africa was entering its final phase. Rommel's forces were being squeezed from both east and west, and must soon collapse. There was already speculation on a leapfrog operation into Sicily, perhaps Italy, but in the meantime thousands of prisoners of war had been accumulated since El Alamein and the landings in French North Africa, and their disposal was becoming a matter of urgency. On this, her outward passage, *Susquehanna*'s caged decks housed a miscellaneous cargo of vehicle spares, PX stores, medical supplies, canned rations and small-calibre ammunition, but on her return she would be carrying 4,000 officers and men of the Afrika Korps.

Captain Felix Mercer had left the bridge with the arrival of the middle watchmen, leaving instructions that he should be roused at 04.00 if nothing untoward occurred in the meantime.

In his diminutive sea-cabin abaft the wheelhouse he peeled off duffelcoat and jacket, eased off his shoes, and decided that this was sufficient disrobing for the next four hours, when *Daemon* would be running the gauntlet of the westerly fringe of the Bay of Biscay. There were probably more U-boats in this area than in any other in the world, departing or homing on their bases at Brest, Lorient, St-Nazaire and La Pallice. Mercer experienced that nagging desire, common to all warship commanders, to remain on the bridge, but he had been on his feet for seventeen hours, and there were penalties for driving oneself too hard. Besides, he wished to avoid displaying the merest suggestion of anxiety. *Daemon*'s reputation and his own record were a sufficiently depressing combination.

Felix Mercer had lost three ships – the first a destroyer off the coast of Norway in 1940 and then his flotilla leader off Crete. On the latter occasion he had barely transferred to his half-leader when that ship, also, had been sent to the bottom. Many men had experienced a sinking, a few had suffered two, but three in less than twelve months had resulted in uneasy calculation among his contemporaries with regard to his next command. There was not the slightest question about Mercer's ability, judgement or courage; it was just that – well, nobody cared to put it into plain words.

Then someone in the Admiralty with an odd sense of humour thought of *Daemon*. There was a certain spiteful logic in making Jonah responsible for the albatross.

Daemon, with a complement of 450, had been built in 1919. She was a D-class light cruiser of 4850 tons, originally mounting six low-angle 6-inch guns and twelve torpedo-tubes; but like others of her vintage she had been designed on principles that had emerged from the First World War, and her weapons were largely irrelevant against the aircraft and submarines of twenty years later. Three 4-inch AA guns and several small-calibre weapons had been added, and thirty depth-charges were stowed in her tiller-flat – a modest concession when even the smaller destroyers carried a hundred. Nothing, however, could be done about her inadequate armour or moderate speed of 29 knots.

Under normal circumstances none of this would have mattered. *Daemon* would have served her fifteen or twenty years, showing the flag and her immaculate brasswork in Hong Kong and Honduras, made goodwill visits to New York and Istanbul, been retired into reserve and from thence to the breaker's yard. War, however, had come too soon.

Daemon was far from alone in her shortcomings. Fully half the Navy's fighting ships were ill-equipped for modern sea warfare, but the confidence of their crews, amounting almost to arrogance, compensated for much during the war's crucial opening period. There was no such confidence in *Daemon*. Her undistinguished career had been puncuated by mishaps. While other ships, like Vian's destroyers, or *Ajax* and *Achilles*, or *Norfolk* and *Suffolk*, had been in the right place at the right time, *Daemon* never had. When opportunities had arisen, something had always seemed to go wrong. She had been the subject of several courts of enquiry, had sent one commander to a court martial, and there had been a suicide. The conviction that she was 'bad joss' was firmly implanted. *Daemon* was a pariah; nobody relished serving in her, or seeing her in company – and now she had Captain Felix Mercer to command her.

Lobby Ludd was the victim of a diabolical injustice – or, when he thought about it, a whole series of injustices. It was the ship's first night at sea, and he had the middle watch. *Daemon* was a 'pusser' ship, and no bleedin' mistake, a ship with a disciplined and meticulous routine that aimed at efficiency but which, by its uncompromising nature and its inescapability, could reduce men to the level of automata. 'An efficient ship', claimed the platitude, 'is a happy ship.' It was probably true, until obsession with efficiency became bloody-minded.

His mess-fellows, from first impressions, were a decent enough shower, a mixed bag of telegraphists, signalmen and coders – Smithie, Knocker White, Jan Prettyman, Steevo, Tug Wilson – but he'd have to watch that bastard of a Master-at-Arms, and the soddin' Chief Yeoman hadn't exactly offered his tot, either . . .

'Tomorrow forenoon,' the Chief Yeoman had instructed, 'after dawn action stations, I want the flag-deck cleaned up proper.' To Lobby Ludd the flag-deck was already alarmingly clinical; it was difficult to imagine what more could be done, unless they all wore bleedin' masks and gowns like bleedin' surgeons. It was bad enough wearing Number Threes. 'O' course, Chief,' he suggested, 'if we 'ad some Mansion Polish, we could make it like the soddin' Palm Court 'Otel, if we 'ad some bleedin' palm-trees.'

The Chief Yeoman had turned narrowed eyes. 'So you're one of them witty ones, are you, Ludd?' He nodded. 'All right. For a start, you can get all the paintwork washed, during the dog watches, and you can sing comic songs quietly while you're doin' it. When you've finished that, there's the twenty-inch to be cleaned and greased, and the Aldis batteries taken down for charging. Then there's the canvas on the flag-locker . . .'

'I've got a photo,' Lobby Ludd told Smithie, and brought it from his locker. 'O' course, it ain't very good of 'er; she's better than this really, but it gives yer an idea.'

'Ah, yes,' Smithie agreed. 'Class. Yer can always tell when a party's got class. Sticks out a mile.' He peered at the photograph more closely, then turned it over. 'Why ain't she writ nothin' on it? I mean – SWALK, or ITALY and HOLLAND?'

Lobby Ludd sniffed. 'We're too bleedin' matchoor fer that sort o' thing. She's a nurse, see – a VAD. Shave off. Like yer said, she's class. Most o' the time she's mixing wi' consultants an' neuro-surgeons – cocktails wi' the Dean o' the Faculty, an' all that shit. Dinner-jackets an' bow-ties—'

The SRE exploded. *'Cooks to the galley. Hands to the mess for rum.'*

Smithie was doubtful. 'Them navy nurses in Dartmouth, when I 'ad that shrapnel, wouldn't bring yer a soddin' bedpan. "Orderlay! Fetch this man a receptacle, will yew?" And if yer rolled a tickler in bed, they looked at yer like yer'd raped a bleedin' nun. I mean, nurses ain't *wimmin.* Jes' fancy puttin' yer leg over – "Has this object been sterilized? 'Ave yer 'ad yer anti-tetanus?" '

'If yer play yer cards right, Nurse McCuddly,' he had informed her, 'I might let yer push my chair ter the ENSA show ternight, see. The eyes o' Aberdeen will be upon yer – the only sailor among teemin' thousands o' pongoes. I was going ter raffle meself, but I decided – as a result of yer devotion ter duty, not ter mention the provocative swing of yer hips as yer dishes out the figs an' custard – that only Nurse McCuddly—'

She was cool. 'My name is McCudden, Mr Ludd, and I have already resigned myself to accompanying you to the concert. I happen to be on stand-by duty. Now' – she drew off his coverlet – 'I have to give you a rub, and I do *not* want suggestions . . .'

There were not thousands, nor even hundreds, at the ENSA concert in the chilly outpatients' reception-hall. There was a scattering of soldiers from Castlehill whose demeanour suggested they were not present by choice, several barrage-balloon men, a group of ATS girls who sat pointedly aloof, whispering, and a dozen interlopers from men's surgical. A shabby placard on the makeshift stage announced 'ENSA presents: Forces' Frolics: A Medley of Melody and Masquerade'. An elderly comedian shouted elderly jokes, stamped his feet, and gave a number of impersonations that stretched the most charitable imagination. The audience brightened momentarily when two leggy young ladies tap-danced and high-kicked to a piano accompaniment, but sank back into apathy at the reappearance of the comedian with a song that advised the females to keep their hands on their ha'pennies. A conjurer in Chinese costume pulled the flags of the Allies out of his mouth, poured milk and flour into a hat and produced a cake, and persuaded two budgerigars to climb a miniature ladder.

Lobby Ludd turned his surreptitious attention to Nurse McCudden. Until now his appreciation of feminine qualities had been confined to the physical, focused upon breasts, buttocks and legs and accompanied by speculation on sexual performance. Indeed, intellect in a woman usually meant a less easy conquest; he could vouch for that. His few sexual adventures had been less than satisfying. In Walham Green, London, there had been Eileen Wilkins, who attended the Fulham Polytechnic and who had been frigidly uncooperative when he had pulled her knickers below her knees. That's what bleedin' education did. And Freda Harris of Wimbledon Park had been a prick-teaser. One day Freda Harris was going to get it, and he hoped it was a big buck nigger on Wimbledon Common on a cold night. Then there had been red-haired Bridie Kelly, in Douglas, who had placidly submitted to being revealingly unbuttoned but declined to lie on the grass because her Sunday dress might be soiled. Dolores in Liverpool hardly counted; he only remembered the bed, her big white breasts and the few seconds of her expectant groping before sinking into intoxicated oblivion. She had been gone by morning.

Nurse McCudden, now, was something different. He ventured upon the usual avenue of speculation, of formulating a mental picture of her naked and waiting with arms lifted as he unlaced his shoes, but the tantalizing vision eluded him. Nurse McCudden refused to be undressed and laid on a sheepskin rug, for his approval. Of course, he reasoned, underneath her starched apron and thermometer she would be much the same as any other woman, give or take an inch. Lobby Ludd concentrated his innocent gaze on the swell of her bodice, but the comedian had stopped shouting, people were rising from their seats and the piano was grinding through the national anthem. Nurse McCudden regarded him resignedly. 'Thirty-six, twenty-six, thirty-eight, Mr Ludd,' she told him. 'I wear camiknickers. I have good legs, and I have a small birthmark just below my left hip. However, since you can only move slowly with two sticks, any further speculation on your part will be wasted. We'll get you tucked into bed with a glass of hot milk and some chloral hydrate.'

He was righteously offended. 'Shave off. A bloke can *think*, can't he?'

She shook her head. 'Not with chloral hydrate he can't.'

two

'No, we tin't exactly engaged,' Lobby Ludd told Smithie. 'Not exactly. It's an understandin', if yer know what I mean.' Smithie seemed unsure, so Lobby Ludd expanded. 'It ain't like picking up some party in Fore Street, mate, jes' fer an 'andful o' sprats in the back row o' the Odeon.' He sniffed. 'There comes a time, see, when yer meet a party, and yer think, "This is my soddin' life partner." Ain't yer ever thought that?' Smithie confessed that he had not; twelve years in the bleedin' Andrew was enough to be going on with. Jan Prettyman, who came from Bovey Tracey, claimed that he had thought that way, once, about a Land Army girl, until she was put in the club by a tractor salesman from Newton Abbot. 'It was the time we 'ad mastitis,' he explained.

'These bleedin' spuds 'ave got mastitis,' Steevo said, peeling the mess potatoes. 'It's them soddin' Wop prisoners o' war that they use on farms. They've got bigger eyes than Eddie bleedin' Cantor. I bet they piss on 'em.' Steevo was an HO – a 'Hostilities Only' rating with a cynical view of every aspect of naval life. It was not that Steevo entertained any inherent hostility towards the Navy, but he had never recovered from the injustice of being prised from a second-hand car business which had just begun to promise a handsome revenue. It was infuriating that, while he was peeling potatoes into a bucket, his Shepherd's Bush rivals were caulking jaded gear-boxes with oil-soaked sawdust and making an easy fortune. 'Bleedin' marvellous,' he snorted. 'Bleedin' marvellous.'

If Lobby Ludd had an understanding with regard to Nurse Fiona McCudden, he was not entirely confident that it was mutual. The cultivation of a serious relationship required time and opportunity, and there had been little of either in the antiseptic setting of the Aberdeen Infirmary. He had not even acquired the photograph by honest means. Of course, he told himself, he had been on the brink of success. In a few more days Nurse McCudden would have melted, but Authority had insisted that Signalman Ludd, ex-*Virtue*, should proceed on three weeks' survivor's leave before reporting himself to RNB Devonport for redrafting. And he had never expected the pier-head jump to *Daemon*. It seemed incredible that, while the barracks teemed with men who awaited a sea-going draft, Signalman Ludd should find himself in a foreign-bound ship within twenty-four hours of arrival.

First, however, there had been three weeks in Walham Green, in the small, shabby sweetshop where his mother battled with coupons and shrinking supplies. 'I can't think what they *do* with all these coupons,' she puzzled. 'They' were the nebulous powers who sent her incomprehensible forms to complete in duplicate, imposed rations, reduced the gas pressure, abolished bananas, crumpets and calf's liver, and put clocks forward two hours for no apparent reason. She had never understood why chickens now only laid one egg per week and sometimes only half an egg, or why, if there was a shortage of pineapple chunks, 'they' simply didn't make more.

Walham Green and North End Road, where, on leave from shore training, he had once swaggered with cap on back of head and the devil-may-care nonchalance of the homecoming sailor, had lost their savour. They had shrunk and grown grey with war weariness. People had developed the facility of shutting out, mentally, the passage of events that were not their immediate, daily concern, and names like Stalingrad, Tripoli, Murmansk and Guadalcanal were of less moment than an extra ounce of cheese or the fortunate purchase of three yards of elastic.

It did not seem fitting, somehow, to tell Mrs Ludd that he had chosen a life partner. She would have said, 'That's very nice, dear,' and then told him that Mrs Arnold's son, Brian – that was the one who played the piano at the wedding, dear – had been called up. The Air Force. And after all that time with the Gas, Light and Coke. Mrs Ludd had nodded absently when he mentioned his two broken legs. Mrs Godber, she said, had broken her ankle once; she *would* polish under the mats. Lobby Ludd refrained from suggesting that Mrs Godber's experience, albeit harrowing, was not quite the same as being torpedoed in the North Sea, as lying frozen and sodden in a Carley float as men choked and died. 'That must have been very nasty, dear,' she would have said.

He was not quite sure how Nurse Fiona McCudden would fit into a Walham Green background; hardly in Mrs Ludd's sweetshop – that was certain. There were, however, problems of higher priority, not least of which was the establishment of his understanding with Nurse McCudden on firmer ground. Well, it hadn't exactly been an understanding. Not exactly.

'If yer like,' he had told her off-handedly as he laced his shoes, 'I'll write to yer.' He had rehearsed his words carefully.

'Yer'll be 'ere, of course – Aberdeen? It ain't any trouble. Letters from HM ships don't need stamps.'

She had been smoothing the coverlet of the bed he had vacated, and he did not see the frown that briefly shadowed her face and then evaporated as quickly. 'I'd like that,' she nodded. 'If I'm not here, I'm sure your letter will be forwarded.' 'Letter', she had said, not 'letters'.

No, he conceded later, it wasn't exactly an understanding, but it was better than a kick up the arse. As Bungy Williams had so rightly pointed out, faint heart never screwed a pig. He wished he could shake off the uneasy feeling that the tranquil and attractive Nurse McCudden was really beyond his reach. He wished he was better educated, and could talk like Coder Crowthorne, who had once been a publisher's proof-reader, and used expressions like 'in the final analysis' and 'notwithstanding the circumstances'. When he reached RNB, he would enquire about the Higher Educational Test. The Navy had bleedin' schoolmaster officers, didn't it? For a start, he could stop soddin' and blindin' . . .

'This afternoon,' Lobby Ludd told Steevo, 'notwithstandin' the circumstances, I'm goin' ter get my 'ead down. In the final analysis, I've got the bleedin' First Dog.' Steevo looked up from the potato he was peeling. 'An' why don't yer go sick?' he enquired.

There had still been stalls in the North End Road, buses with methane-gas trailers, off-ration rabbit, mutton selling for lamb, and doubtful sausages, utility stockings, strange cigarette brands, black-out torches, stick-on soles and remoulded tyres, powdered egg, queues for oranges, for whalemeat, for children's shoes. Policemen were stunted by steel helmets. There were barrage balloons, surface shelters, water tanks, sandbags, and Elsie and Doris Waters at the old Granville Theatre. Owen Melville, of the Borough Engineer's Department, descended the dusty steps of the Town Hall. 'Why, hello – er . . .' He frowned. 'Hello. Home on leave again? My word, I wish I was in the Navy.' He chuckled. 'Still, we're always glad to see you lads. When do you go back?' He did not wait for an answer.

'Sorry – I must fly. Staff canteen committee, y'know – Deputy Clerk ...' He had gone.

The bar of the Britannia was thronged with midday drinkers – a bus driver, workmen in overalls, old ladies with glasses of stout, old men playing cribbage, and a young man in seaman's uniform, talking.

'O' course,' he was saying, as Lobby Ludd entered, 'this civvy rum ain't the same as yer get in the Navy. When yer've drunk navy rum fer a few years, this stuff's nothing. When yer on Russian convoys, I can tell yer' – he sniffed – 'yer need the real thing ...' From the clumsy cut of his suit, his boots and his unfaded jean collar, the young man was enjoying his first leave from a shore training establishment.

'Wotcher, Townie,' Lobby Ludd nodded. 'What's the buzz?' The other nodded back, unspeaking, suddenly interested in a door marked 'Gentlemen'. Lobby Ludd called for a pint of beer.

'What yer were saying about being torpedoed,' the bus driver said. 'What's it feel like? I mean, suppose yer can't swim?'

Lobby Ludd's eyes widened. 'Shave off. Yer was tinfished?' He nodded gravely. 'I might 'ave guessed them clothes was survivor's kit. No matelot would wear clobber like that unless he was a survivor or a bleedin' nozzer jes' joined.'

The young seaman drained his glass, coughed, glanced at the clock. 'Is that the right time?' he enquired.

'They ain't piped "cooks ter the galley yet",' Lobby Ludd said. ''Ave another grog, mate. Navy size? Yer can knock this stuff back in one. Where did yer get shamfered?'

'Shamfered—?'

'Ah, don't tell me, mate. Walls 'ave bleedin' ears.' He leaned forward confidentially. 'I thought I recognized yer, when I came in. Didn't I see yer in Guzz, in the drill-shed, when *Virtue*'s lot was drawing their loan bedding?'

'Guzz—?'

'I thought so. Shave off.' He sucked his teeth. 'If I 'adn't recognized yer, I might 'ave thought yer was some green sprog up from *Collingwood*, swinging the lamps like a bleedin' three-badger, full o' flannel.' He sighed. '*Virtue*, did yer say? Roll on. Them soddin' V and Ws are hard ships, all right. I've 'eard it's corned dog and 'ard tack, watch-and-watch about, and bleedin' salt-water dhobeyin'. Is that right?'

'Well,' the other agreed, 'as a matter of fact—'

'The funny thing is,' Lobby Ludd frowned, 'judging by the number of blokes that sez they're survivors, *Virtue* must have 'ad a bigger ship's company than the bleedin' *Rodney*. I don't know where they all stowed their soddin' 'ammocks. Shave off. I 'ad an old mate in *Virtue*. Name o' Williams – Bungy Williams. And there was a bloke named Albright. Yer *must* 'ave known Stripey Albright—'

The young seaman had difficulty in remembering the names, but he did remember that he had a pressing appointment in Hammersmith. 'Tell 'em on the bus yer a survivor,' was Lobby Ludd's parting advice, 'and yer won't 'ave ter pay.'

'When yer think about it,' the bus driver considered, 'we don't know arf of what goes on.'

'Too true, mate.' Lobby Ludd agreed. 'Yer could write a bleedin' book.' He finished his beer and left, paused outside the Fulham Polytechnic to light a cigarette, and found himself confronted by Freda Harris.

'Why, Charlie Ludd!' she exclaimed. 'How did you know I finished at twelve-thirty?' She wrinkled her nose. 'You've been making enquiries.' Freda Harris was brunette, vivacious, and with those provocative physical qualities that unfailingly kindled male speculation, but Lobby Ludd had learned to be cautious with regard to Freda.

'Ah, yes,' he nodded. 'I read yer case in the *News o' the World* – "Girl Student Foils Advances with Galvanized Bloomers"...'

'Charlie!' she chided coquettishly, and took his arm. 'You're just sulking because you didn't have it off with me after the Civil Defence social evening. You could hardly *expect* it, the first time you met me. And I did say *next* time.' She matched her pace to his and snuggled closer. 'I heard about your accident—'

'Accident!' he snorted. 'Shave off. When a ship gets belted up the bracket by two tinfish, it ain't an accident!'

She was contrite. 'But you're all right now, Charlie, aren't you? Your injuries, I mean – they didn't—?'

'It was my *legs* I broke,' he gritted.

'Well, there you are, then,' she told him. 'There's no problem, is there? And after your long rest you ought to be boiling over.' She rolled her eyes. 'You couldn't have got much while you had two broken legs, Charlie.'

Lobby Ludd simmered. He had travelled this avenue on a previous occasion, and been deluged with icy water at the end of it. Freda Harris was one of those calculating females who delighted in arousing sexual excitement in a partner but had not the slightest intention of satisfying it. There was a name for her sort, and Lobby Ludd had no desire to be snared again. On the other hand, Freda Harris was a luscious temptation. There was always a first time. *Someone* had to make it, sooner or later.

'The last time,' he reminded her, 'I got as far as yer garden gate, and then I 'ad ter walk four miles 'ome. Yer said that if I felt randy I oughter pour cold water over it.' He shrugged. 'That's what yer get fer trustin' someone.'

Freda Harris giggled. 'Well, you did insist on taking me home.' She considered. 'Why don't you meet me in Wimbledon, Charlie? There's *Hellzapoppin'* at the Astoria – and then you needn't miss the last train. I promise I won't leave you at the garden gate, or tell you to tie a knot in it.' She squeezed his arm. 'I can't say for certain, but you might find it was worth waiting for.'

At the Astoria a newsreel had shown tanks, dust, and soldiers with upraised thumbs in North Africa, aircraft dropping bombs on Hamburg, American soldiers chewing gum 'somewhere in England', and elderly Home Guards throwing petrol bombs. If Hitler still thought he could invade England, crowed the commentator, then just let him try. The film *Hellzapoppin'* proved largely unintelligible to Lobby Ludd, who, he might have agreed later, gave it little attention. He was more concerned with the buttons of Freda Harris's blouse, which seemed to be fastened by rivets, and the junction of her stockinged thighs, which were welded together. Here and now, Freda whispered, were neither the place nor time, and the two white-haired ladies in the seats in front, who shot shocked glances over their shoulders and conferred in equally shocked hisses, obviously agreed. The Astoria, Lobby Ludd concluded, was a soddin' dead loss.

It was dusk and just beginning to drizzle with rain when they reached the street of houses and neat gardens in Wimbledon Park where, on that earlier occasion, his expectations had been deflated. The Harris house was darkened and silent. '*Now*, Charlie,' Freda said, 'you haven't really been a gentleman, but I did promise. You can come in, but *don't* make a noise.'

'It don't make much noise,' Lobby Ludd calculated. He was still suspicious. 'Where's yer parents?'

'It's their night for the old people's whist,' she explained, and led him into an immaculately furnished sitting-room that smelled of polish and middle-class respectability. There was an electric fire with artificial logs, and on a gleaming sideboard stood a porcelain shepherdess and a folded copy of *The Times*. It was very different from the gloomy little room in Walham Green, where every available space was occupied by cartons of Gold Flake and Ogden's St Bruno, Fry's chocolate creams, and piles of unsold newspapers awaiting return. Lobby looked around guardedly for an ashtray.

'What do yer do with yer fag-ends?' he asked. 'Swaller 'em?' He drew Freda to a settee, but she wriggled free.

'I'll switch the fire on, Charlie,' she said, and did. 'It takes a few minutes to warm up. Do you want to go upstairs to do anything?'

'No,' he replied, and drew her to the settee again. 'No wonder I couldn't undo these buttons in the dark. They ain't buttons, they're 'ooks.' He slid a hand under her bra. 'Now them's what I call buds,' he approved. Freda Harris looked at the clock. 'If you'd like some coffee first, Charlie,' she suggested breathlessly, 'it won't take long ...'

Lobby Ludd was absorbed in the awkward but agreeable task of lowering Freda's knickers – awkward because Freda was less than cooperative, and agreeable because this, Lobby Ludd told himself, was *it*. At a time like this, who needed coffee? Charles Boyer never took coffee. There was simply a fade-out, and everyone knew exactly what had happened when they next saw him rebuttoning his shirt.

'It's funny how yer can be mistaken about people,' he said, groping at his trouser-flap, but there was an interruption – the rattle of a door, and voices. Lobby Ludd froze, and Freda struggled upright, frantically, relieved.

'My goodness, Charlie—!' She wrenched her skirt down. 'They must have finished early!' Lobby Ludd choked on a profanity, incensed, but knew himself defeated. When Mr and Mrs Harris entered, Freda was seated on the piano-stool with her legs demurely crossed.

'We're a little late, dear,' Mr Harris boomed, then smiled at Lobby Ludd. 'Good evening, young man. Have we met before?' He was short, rotund, with a bald head liberally freckled and a small, sandy moustache. He wore a clerical collar. A diminutive Mrs Harris hovered behind him, drawing out a hat-pin, and Freda rose dutifully from the piano-stool, eyes lowered. 'I'll make the coffee, Daddy, while you talk to Charlie. He's a survivor. He's been torpedoed.'

Mr Harris's hand was podgy and warm. 'My dear boy,' he sympathized. 'I know *exactly* how you feel.' Lobby Ludd doubted it. 'Sometimes it helps to talk about it,' Mr Harris added encouragingly, but Lobby Ludd shook his head and shrugged, baring his teeth in a smile. 'I know,' Mr Harris nodded. 'I know exactly.'

Freda brought the coffee and resumed her seat on the piano-stool.

'Time is a great healer,' Mr Harris assured him. 'It's a pity you have to dash off, Charlie. You must come again. Freda, you must bring Charlie again.' He frowned at the clock. 'No, no – I'm not rushing you off, dear boy. Finish your coffee before you go. You must come earlier next time.' He rose to his feet, humming. 'Freda, dear – you'll lock up when Charlie goes? Good, good.' He beamed at Lobby Ludd, and left the door of the sitting-room open. Lobby listened to his footsteps slowly ascending the stairs.

Freda sighed. 'Wasn't it *maddening*, Charlie? No' – she held up a hand – 'it's no good. He won't go to sleep until he's heard the door being shut and bolted. If he doesn't, he'll give us just five minutes before he comes down for his glasses, and then he'll stay to read *The Times* editorial.' She smiled wistfully.

'But there's always another time, Charlie. You may not believe it, but I'm just as frustrated as you are. And you've got that long walk again.' She led the way into the hall and opened the front door. 'When I think what you're going to do to me next time' – she shivered deliciously – 'I just can't wait!'

Lobby Ludd said nothing. He closed the door firmly, waited for a moment, then shot home the bolts. Freda's eyes widened in disbelief. 'Charlie!' she whispered. He put a finger to his lips, took her elbow, and led her on tiptoe to the sitting-room they had just left. Freda shook her head vigorously, but he shut this door also and, for good measure, quietly turned the key in the lock. Then he beckoned Freda to the settee.

Freda glanced apprehensively at the ceiling and then at Lobby Ludd. He beckoned again, grimly, and she sat nervously on the edge of the settee. 'Charlie,' she whispered helplessly, 'if he hears—'

He had already removed her blouse. 'He won't,' he assured her, 'unless yer start screamin' wi' unbridled passion.' He unbuttoned his trousers. 'Now, if yer think yer goin' ter be shocked, shut yer eyes.'

She was shocked. 'Charlie,' she pleaded, 'I didn't really mean what I said. I'm not really like that, Charlie. You wouldn't want to take advantage of me, would you?' But he already had. 'Charlie!' she gasped. 'I'm a virgin!'

'You *was* a virgin,' he gritted, 'but yer don't 'ave ter worry about it any more. Shave off. Think o' the years yer've waited.'

Daemon had paused for only hours at Gibraltar, to discharge mail and to embark a handful of passengers from the local establishment, HMS *Rooke*, bound for Malta.

'We are proceeding directly to Malta,' Captain Mercer informed his ship's company over the address system, 'and we shall be crossing the enemy's shipping routes between Tunisia and Sicily. The Afrika Korps is facing defeat in North Africa, but the Germans are still fighting bitterly, and supplies and reinforcements are still being ferried in to support their Mareth Line. To achieve this they are utilizing every possible type of vessel – warships, freighters, and even motorized sailing ships. Sooner or later, however, the German–Italian front must collapse, and then traffic will be in the opposite direction, from Cap Bon to Sicily. Every enemy transport sunk, therefore, will weaken the enemy in either Tunisia or Italy.

'We shall maintain first state of readiness for the entire period at sea.' Even the most modest action, successfully concluded, would help to dissolve his crew's pessimistic opinion of their ship. Mercer would settle for an Italian sardine-boat.

Twenty minutes after slipping their moorings, with Gibraltar's eastward face still in sight astern, *Daemon* was overhauled by the fast cruiser-minelayer *Swiftsure*, working up to forty knots and with her boiler-fans audible almost a mile away. A bugle trilled, and *Swiftsure*'s ensign dipped in salute as she forged past and ahead with nonchalant ease, while envious eyes watched her from the older ship. The Abdiel-class cruiser had everything that *Daemon* lacked: a powerful appearance, twin-turreted guns, a sustained speed that outpaced anything else in the Navy, and even accommodation for 240 mines – accommodation that was now crammed with war supplies for Malta. *Swiftsure* was capable of reaching Malta and then returning to Gibraltar before *Daemon* had completed the first leg of the passage. 'Sorry I cannot keep you company,' her lamp chuckled, 'but will tell them you are coming and to double up on fenders.' Mercer made no comment, and Commander Joe Plummer, his second-in-command, only grunted.

The Chief Yeoman lowered his telescope. 'She sank an Italian destroyer and two small freighters in a night action last week, only five miles off the Sicilian coast.' He turned. 'Ludd! When you're sent aft to dip the ensign, you'll *double*, see.'

'Sorry, Chief,' Lobby Ludd apologized. 'I'll remember next time.' He had remembered this bleedin' time, but that bastard of a Master-at-Arms had halted him in his tracks with an angry bellow. 'Ludd! I don't know where you think yer going, but yer'll *walk*, see. This is the upper deck, not bloody Aintree!'

The cold green of the Mediterranean had become ink-blue, crested with silver, the sky cloudless, but there was a chilling wind, and the night watchkeepers were grateful for the duffel-coats they had earlier stowed away. At dawn, *Daemon*'s radar reported aircraft approaching from the southward at 250 knots. The action alarm hammered, but the three aircraft that roared low and fast over the ship were Hurricanes that circled once and then turned away, satisfied, toward the eastward horizon.

The muzzles of the 4-inch HA guns followed, sniffing the air. 'Secure,' Mercer ordered. 'Revert to first state.' No warship commander relished an enemy air attack but, just this once, he wished those had been three Luftwaffe aircraft.

It was at dusk on that second day, as the first watch duty-men closed up, that the enemy report was received on area broadcast. *'Immediate Air reconnaissance report. One enemy cruiser and seven unidentified vessels position 38.55N 09.20E. Course 145. Speed 12 knots. Time of origin 19.26b/16.'*

Mercer came to the bridge. 'A cruiser and *seven* unidentified vessels? Do these RAF types know what an enemy cruiser looks like?' He frowned. 'Pilot.'

The Navigating Officer, Lieutentant Cotton, was already at the chart-table, working in the small pool of light that the shaded lamp afforded. He glanced up. 'Whatever they are, sir, they're on a course from Cagliari to Bizerta. Assuming they maintain that course, and assuming the RAF know what twelve knots are, we can intercept in about four hours – say, midnight – although we'll have them on radar before then, converging. We can't miss an armada like that.' He almost added, 'Not even *Daemon*,' but checked.

The Captain nodded. 'Number One, bring us up to full speed, please. Pilot, let's have that interception course, at the rush. I want to know *immediately* we have radar contact so that we can come around to the same course as the enemy. Perhaps we can do a Matapan.' Two years before, Admiral Cunningham's squadron had pounced from the Mediterranean night to pulverize three 8-inch cruisers and two destroyers, with the Italian ships caught with their guns still trained fore and aft. 'A cruiser and *seven* unidentified vessels,' Mercer repeated, musingly. 'Seven *what*?'

'If they're seven destroyers,' Commander Plummer smiled quietly, 'or even seven E-boats, we'll be in the cactus.' With only six open 6-inch guns, her thin plating and modest speed, *Daemon* was likely to find herself inferior to almost any enemy cruiser and, if the latter were supported, an engagement could be suicidal.

'There should be an amplifying report,' Mercer decided. 'The enemy force can't be more than an hour's flying-time from an American or British airfield.' There were torpedo-carrying Barracudas and Beauforts, American Corsairs and Avengers, all within strike range, while submarines from Malta's 10th Flotilla were deployed in the area. It was inconceivable that the enemy, now pin-pointed, would be left free from attack for the four hours necessary for *Daemon* to reach him.

An hour passed into two. *Daemon*'s decks vibrated as her turbines drove her through the sea at twenty-eight knots, her funnels, with paint roasting, vomiting smoke blacker than the night. The Senior Engineer watched the needles of his gauges climb steadily, knowing that 40,000 shaft horse-power was devouring 15 tons of fuel an hour, that his elderly engines were being punished as they seldom had before. There was no amplifying radio report, only two broadcast repetitions of the original signal. At 22.30 Mercer ordered hands to change into clean underclothes and, a half-hour later, sent them to quarters.

'Radar to bridge. Surface echoes, range approximately twenty miles, relative bearing oh-two-oh.' The voice from the small loudspeaker-grille was that of Lieutenant Joyce, Radar Officer, who was probably standing at his operator's shoulder. On the bridge there was sudden silence. *'It could be two or more vessels – moving north–south – but we'll need a few more minutes, sir.'*

'Keep me informed, please, Joyce. I'd like the contact's course and speed as soon as possible,' Mercer ordered. 'Bring us around to southward, Pilot. Reduce to twenty knots. All positions closed up, Guns?'

'All positions closed up and checked, sir, ready to load.'

'Thank you. A gun, load star-shell, please; the remainder CPBC. All guns broadsides.' Common Pointed Ballistic Capped – 6-inch shells weighing 112 pounds projected by thirty pounds of cordite.

Mercer's face was expressionless. 'As soon as we know a little more, Pilot, I want to be on a twenty-degree converging course.' *Daemon* would have all six of her guns firing to port and, if the action were prolonged, the dawn sky would flush behind the target, placing the enemy at a disadvantage – unless the enemy was an 8-inch cruiser with radar, in which case *Daemon* would never get within range. The enemy could be watching the British ship's approach even now, with guns loaded and waiting—

'Radar to bridge. Echoes suggest close-formed group of vessels, none large. Relative bearing three-one-five, course one-five-five, speed ten knots – range about thirteen miles and closing.'

None large? Mercer frowned slightly. 'Chief Yeoman, hoist another ensign, please.' *Daemon* was to fly a battle-flag for the first time. 'Ah, Commander, let the ship know on SRE what's happening, will you? We expect to engage in about thirty minutes, if the target's what we think it is.'

'Director to bridge. Gunnery radar has target on screen. Bearing two-eight-oh, range eighteen thousand and closing.'

'We'll get just a little closer,' Mercer said, and then turned as someone shouted.

'Gun-flashes, sir! Almost dead abeam, to port!'

'Main W/T to bridge! Enemy report from Swiftsure *to C-in-C Med. One destroyer, seven unidentified vessels bearing three-five-oh, range two miles, course one-five-five. My position—'*

'*Swiftsure*!' Someone else swore. 'At two miles' range? Christ! The sod must have turned back—'

'At forty knots,' Mercer snapped. 'Full speed ahead both. Port ten.' The Coxswain's acknowledgement and the clang-clang of the telegraphs came from the wheelhouse voice-pipe. *Daemon* heeled as she turned her bows towards the pale flashes that flickered on the eastern horizon. 'Midships. Steady. Steer oh-nine-oh. Director, stand by, please.' He was coldly angry.

'All guns load, load, load.'

'All guns ready.'

It was damn silly, he knew, charging like a mad bull into an unknown battle situation, but he needed a sop for his frustration, his choking feeling that he was being robbed. He knew what had happened. *Swiftsure*, far eastward of the reported enemy's position, had wheeled about, had made contact, had challenged, and then opened fire at almost point-blank range.

It hadn't been an enemy cruiser, only a destroyer – no match for *Swiftsure*, whose captain had gone straight into an attack while Mercer had wasted time, jockeying for position.

'Looks like a hit, sir.' Ahead, in the darkness, a flame-coloured puffball swelled suddenly, then as quickly shrank, dulled to red.

'Radar to bridge. Target echoes are breaking up, sir, eight miles dead ahead. If it's Swiftsure *firing, she's bearing oh-two-oh, ten miles, on a reciprocal course, closing at twenty knots—'*

'Director to bridge. Ranging by radar, sir – eighteen thousand and closing. Ready to fire.' The voice was mildly reproachful. All binoculars were levelled ahead at the distant gun-flashes. 'Eleven-second salvoes, sir,' someone calculated. 'That's *Swiftsure*'s four-sevens.' Nobody disputed it.

Mercer turned. 'Chief Yeoman, flash a challenge, please. *Swiftsure* must have us on her screen by now, and she should read your lamp. We don't want to be firing at each other.' But that was exactly what he felt like doing. *Daemon* had bungled it again. 'Come around to south-west, Pilot.'

'C-in-C Med from *Swiftsure* repeated Admty, VA Malta, *Daemon*: Immediate: My 162305b. One Pessagno-class destroyer and seven Siebelfahrein ferries engaged and sunk in position 37.55N 09.45E. Each ferry carrying two Mark VI Tiger tanks presumably consigned Bizerta. Am picking up survivors and have now been joined by *Daemon*. Further signal follows.'

Lobby Ludd had turned the twenty-inch lamp to the sky to flash the challenging letters, changed every four hours, and *Swiftsure* had responded correctly, adding, 'I thought you were somewhere around. Sorry have not left you much but will give you halfway start next time.' Mercer grunted.

'You can take that battle ensign down, Ludd,' the Chief Yeoman said, 'before anyone sees it.'

'If I fold it up careful,' Lobby Ludd agreed, 'we might get our money back, sale or return.

three

Blond-haired Gunther Jensen, First Lieutenant of U-157 and a product of the Hitler Youth movement, was becoming increasingly impatient with the apparent lack of urgency in his commanding officer's philosophy. Captain Behrmann was one of the old school of German naval officers who, in Jensen's opinion, had been unable to adapt to the concept of total war, who believed there were rules of behaviour, and who were even capable of speaking with respectful admiration for the British Navy, the detested enemy. Behrmann, of course, had met British officers in Kiel and Portsmouth before the war, and he incensed Jensen with his shrugging scepticism towards the news bulletins from Berlin. The British, Behrmann always said, were not that stupid. If they were, they could not have survived the last three years of unremitting disasters that Goebbels' ministry claimed. Men like Behrmann should be behind desks, not commanding submarines in the vicious war of the Atlantic.

U-157 had reached St-Nazaire from the Baltic without incident, and for two weeks had been moored in the semi-darkness of an immense concrete bunker with a roof seven metres thick that no bomb could penetrate. The British had tried, repeatedly, devastating the surrounding dockyard area, but their heaviest missiles had done no more than raise a little dust inside the submarine haven. Jensen fretted to be at sea; he had hardly controlled his anger when the Captain had declined to attack the British cruiser west of Ushant, and now Behrmann showed no anxiety to be at sea again. Every function of the submarine's machinery had been meticulously adjusted, instruments recalibrated, torpedoes checked, and both screws had been removed for the shafts to be rebushed because, Behrmann had decided, they were too noisy – although Jensen had noticed nothing unusual. 'When you're three thousand miles from home, Jensen,' Behrmann said, 'with a bearing running hot or a tail-shaft fractured, it's no damned use wishing for a dry dock. And you can't claim a replay when a torpedo malfunctions and a destroyer's roaring down on you at thirty-five knots. That's when you wish you'd checked everything thoroughly before you started.' He had smiled. 'Don't worry, Jensen. The British aren't going to run away. There'll be enough of them for you, once we get started.'

Half of U-157's ratings had never previously been outside Baltic waters – an uncomfortable but unavoidable percentage. German shipyards were building submarines faster than they were being lost, but trained crewmen could not be produced so quickly. Almost all of the élite personnel that had begun the war had now gone, killed or captured, and they included many of Germany's ace submarine commanders. Gunther Prien, who had sunk *Royal Oak* in Scapa Flow, and Joachim Schepke and Otto Kretschmer, who had each claimed the destruction of 200,000 tons of Allied shipping, had all been lost during the space of ten days in March 1941. The British had become more expert, and ships equipped specifically for submarine-hunting were increasingly joining a contest that was crucially balanced. In the spring of 1943 the Germans had deployed 112 of their 240 operational U-boats in the North Atlantic, with the battle against them maintained almost wholly by the British and Canadian navies; only two per cent of escorting vessels were American.

Except for the submarine pens, the port of St-Nazaire was a shambles. Weeds flourished among acres of rusted railway lines torn crazily by high explosives. Roads were pitted with craters hastily filled, and there was hardly a building that was not scarred and patched, hardly a window with glass or a roof fully tiled. Several hulks lay waterlogged in the basin. Concrete and sandbagged emplacements sheltered AA guns, and steel-helmeted sentries watched the gangs of French and conscripted foreign workers. There were high levels of pilfering, and U-157's midshipman, Ehlert, checked every kilogram of dry stores loaded – fresh vegetables, coffee, bread, sausages, bacon, lemons for Vitamin C, powdered egg, sauerkraut, canned meats and milk, soap, sardines. Submarine crews' rations were incomparably superior to those of civilians in the occupied territories, few of whom had seen real coffee or white flour for years. The civilian workers had to be carefully watched, not only with regard to theft, but also for sabotage – the handful of sand, the severed cable, the loosened bolt – which could disable a submarine as surely as an enemy depth-charge.

Jensen would have had every Frenchman stripped and searched at the end of each day, but Behrmann had forbidden it. A few dried peas, a tin or two of condensed soup – what were these when balanced against the hate that reprisals generated? Live and let live. Behrmann was a soft fool.

There were sleazy bars and brothels in St-Nazaire, a dilapidated officers' club, or the casino in La Baule. The veterans of U-157 like Behrmann were in no hurry to get to sea. They had been before. Braun the Chief Engineer, Katter the Quartermaster and Merker the Coxswain were the only crewmen who had served since 1939; they drank themselves to near-insensibility every night and staggered aboard, blaspheming. The younger men, not yet blooded, talked loudly among themselves, but not when the old sweats were present, and there was a nervousness in their bragging. They talked to bolster their courage. There would be photographers, and flowers, and a band braying on the jetty when they slipped their moorings, but out there in the cold, grey Atlantic the filthy Brits were waiting. Braun and Katter and Merker, old men before they were thirty, and living on their nerves, never bragged.

Susquehanna was moored against the mile-long sea-wall of Mers-el-Kebir, westward of Oran, under a hot sun. It was a long tramp for the shuffling groups of German prisoners, and they showed all the signs of utter weariness. Many were unshaven, all were dirty, with broken boots, eyes red-rimmed and skins blotched. They carried haversacks and water-bottles, and they eyed the ship morosely. An American ship? Did that mean they were going to America? There were American troops on the jetty, both white and negro, but there was a whispered rumour, flung back along the trudging column, that the guards on the transport were Poles – and they all knew what that meant.

They were men of the Heeresgruppe Afrika – of 10th, 15th and 21st Panzer Divisions, the Barenthin Regiment, the Koch Storm Regiment, and dozens of other units of which some had fought British, Australians and New Zealanders for two years, had reached Egypt, and then had been forced back, mile by bitter mile, to the Mareth Line in Tunisia. BBC news bulletins claimed that General Feldmarschall Rommel had abandoned the Afrika Korps three weeks before, on 9 March, and had gone to Berlin, but there was no official statement; most men did not want to believe it. The British and American armies, closing from east and west respectively, had not yet linked. With Rommel, there was always hope. If only they had been given a few of the new Tiger Panzers that were being sent by the hundred to the Russian front, they might have halted the American-built Shermans. If only they had been reinforced. If only they had more aircraft. If only . . .

At each of several gangways, Swedish Red Cross personnel were distributing oranges and cigarettes as the long files of dusty men passed. There were more Red Cross officials aboard, watching as the men were checked on embarkation lists, given disinfectant soap, and herded forward, aft and below to bath-spaces. Polish guards stood at the foot and head of every ladder, at every passageway intersection. It was cooler below, and ventilation-fans hummed.

The captured Germans had been embarking for several days, and the earlier arrivals had already discovered that the conditions of detention were far from harsh. Many of them, for months, had been on short rations, usually Italian – sardines in oil, poor bread but no potatoes, canned meat-sausage and tough Italian beef marked with the initials 'AM' – which the Germans decided meant 'Alter Mann', or tinned old man. In *Susquehanna* the food was immeasurably superior. There was fresh white bread, coffee, spam and corned beef, ample potatoes. Only U-boat crews got those sorts of victuals. Americans seemed to waste more food than the Germans had been accustomed to eat. Fresh water was abundant, even hot showers. Compared with the heat and dust of Libya, the flies and stink, the freezing nights and the maiming shrapnel day after vicious day, *Susquehanna* was a luxurious haven, and if American prison camps were the same, then perhaps capture would be tolerable.

Among the four hundred German officers distributed among

the dozens of partitioned cabins that had once carried holiday-makers to Palm Beach and Miami there were mixed opinions. They included twelve generals and more than thirty colonels in addition to staff officers and junior ranks. Separated from their batmen, they had been compelled to carry their own baggage – which meant abandoning most of it – to queue for meals with plates in hand like common soldiers, and to be mustered for roll-call on the boat-deck twice daily under the cold eyes of the Polish guards. Lieutenant-General Kleinschmidt, the senior officer, had protested formally to the American commandant, Colonel Dunlop, but Dunlop had equally formally declined any concessions. 'I am sorry, Herr General, but your conditions of detention are strictly in accordance with the Geneva Convention, and are probably better than those you extend to your own prisoners of war.' It was true, Kleinschmidt knew.

'May I be permitted to know our destination, Colonel?' he enquired. 'Probably half the native population of Oran already knows.'

Dunlop hesitated, then nodded. 'We shall be escorted as far as Gibraltar, and will then proceed to Norfolk, Virginia. After that, I don't know. I guess you'll be segregated and maybe entrained for the Mid-West.' He smiled. 'I don't think you'll have a tough time in Kansas, General.'

Better by far a prisoner of the Americans than of the Russians, Kleinschmidt agreed, and it could not be for long, whichever way the war went. The North African campaign, he knew, was lost, but Europe was a fortress, and the Americans would never face the cost of invasion. They had their hands full in the Pacific. Without the Americans, the British could only fight defensively. No, if the Russian front could be stabilized, there would be a negotiated peace. Nobody – least of all the Americans – would relish an Armageddon that might cost millions of lives.

'When do we leave, Colonel?' he asked.

'As soon as we have embarked our full complement of about four thousand, General, which should be by the end of the week.' The routeing instructions that sent *Susquehanna* through the Straits of Gibraltar were unusual. Troopships and transports had usually embarked at Alexandria and proceeded eastwards, through the Suez Canal and Red Sea, and around the Cape, but there was now less enemy activity in the western Mediterranean and the shorter route was justified. The Atlantic could be dangerous, but *Susquehanna* would steam southward, as far as Parallel 25, to avoid the U-boat concentrations, and her speed would do the rest.

A dry breeze warmed by the desert was blowing off shore as *Daemon* moved slowly through the channel into the inner harbour with the calm water peeling gently away from her bows like torn blue silk. On her bridge, immaculate in white, Captain Mercer raised his binoculars to scan the dun-coloured shoreline of the ten-mile bay, then the jetties and derricks between Cap Falcon and Point Canastral. Somewhere against the piled rocks of the sea-wall, the chart said, was the wreck of the French battleship *Bretagne*, which, with *Provence* and *Dunkerque*, had been 'neutralized' by the Royal Navy's 15-inch guns in July 1940. It was hot – hotter than Grand Harbour. Well, he decided, nothing much could happen here. He felt like crossing his fingers, but that would be a juvenile gesture for a captain RN. *Daemon* had come from Devonport to Gibraltar, then Malta, and now Mers-el-Kebir without a worrying incident – not counting *Swiftsure*.

'There she is, Number One.' He pointed. '*Susquehanna*. It looks as though she's still embarking.'

The big American transport, painted over-all grey, lay at the lighthouse end of the sea-wall. *Susquehanna* was not a graceful ship. She had been built with two funnels, but one of these had been a dummy to make her outline more imposing and symmetrical, and in happier days had housed a children's play-space. Now it was removed, with a result that was not visually pleasing. Of 19,000 tons and 530 feet in length, she was too big, Mercer mused, to have been brought into a combat zone while the situation was still unresolved. She had no guns, no armour plate, and, he would guess, carried a lot of wooden panelling, temporary decks and bulkheads within her. Mercer wondered if she had adequate lifeboats and rafts for the accommodation of 4,000, but presumably the US Maritime Commission knew its business.

Escort *Susquehanna* from Mers-el-Kabir to Gibraltar, ordered C-in-C Med, adhering as closely to the Moroccan coast as was consistent with safety and with the avoidance of Spanish territorial waters. Well, Gibraltar was only 250 miles to the westward. It was the second part of the orders that gave more concern. *Following refuelling at Gibraltar, continue with* Susquehanna *on her south-westerly route as far as Latitude 25.* That meant U-boat waters – not as hazardous, perhaps, as the more northerly Atlantic, but a hunting-ground for the Germans' long-range submarines – and *Daemon* was not the ideal choice for an anti-submarine role. Mercer hoped that *Susquehanna* could live up to her twenty knots.

'It's the "island o' smells an' bells",' Lobby Ludd told Smithie. That was what Stripey Albright had said. The dirty water of Grand Harbour lapped against the worn stonework of the Marino Pinto and Lascaris Wharf. *Daemon* lay moored with her bows towards St Angelo and the harbour entrance, around her lowered side-ladder a scattering of gondola-like *dghaisas.* She was exposed; it was impossible to hide a light cruiser, but the air attacks of the previous year that had littered Grand Harbour, Sliema and Marsa Muscetto creeks with sunken wrecks had become fewer and less intense. There had not been a sixty-plus enemy attack for a week.

'An' rum, buggery an' the lash,' Smithie nodded. That was how Churchill had described the Navy's motivations, and the lower deck spat the phrase defiantly at those pietists who expected men to fight and die, but out of sight and earshot. 'After a week in that two-funnelled bastard we'll start with the bleedin' rum, and come ter the bum later.'

Daemon's libertymen dispersed noisily towards the terrace of small, dingy bars that skirted the jetty. In the musty gloom of Mary's Bar a fat and aged Mary served warm Blue Label bottled beer, perspiring, cranked the handle of an Italian gramophone and told her customers that she had a son in Swansea who owned a café. Spiro, she said. Did they know him? They regretted they did not. She scratched a moist armpit. She could do them fried-egg sandwiches, or steak. Well, not *beef* steak ... They repaired next door, to the Dreadnought.

Daemon had been met off Fifla Island by a tug and led through Malta's searched channel, past the breakwater and the dun-coloured ramparts of Fort Ricasoli and St Angelo. She had begun to off-load mail and stores immediately. The island had survived the lean days of the Axis siege, but supplies by any means were still welcome – by submarine, by the forty-knot cruiser-minelayers *Manxman* and *Welshman*, by convoys fought through from Gibraltar. Malta had also been deprived of an important source of income – the battleships, cruisers, carriers and destroyers that had poured thousands of blue-jackets, with pockets jingling, into the streets of Valetta, Floriana and Sliema. There were soldiers, a few RAF men, but fewer sailors than Malta had entertained for years – only the shore-based ratings of Lascaris and Hal-Far, submariners from the 10th Flotilla in Lazaretto, the crews of two disabled and camouflage-netted destroyers in the side-waters of Parlatorio, and now *Daemon*.

In the Dreadnought, to the music of another hand-cranked gramophone, Lobby Ludd and Smithie experimented with locally made *ambite*, which, Lobby told Smithie, was Maltese for essence of pig-shit. Smithie eyed a fly-encrusted flypaper that hung from the dirty ceiling. 'O' course,' he suggested, 'if yer *fancy* 'er—'

'Fancy 'oo?' Lobby asked.

'Mary, next door. Yer could put a bag over her 'ead. Think of all them egg sandwiches.' They moved further along the jetty to the Movement Inn, for Australian brandy that tasted suspiciously like naval rum.

A policeman was urinating among the rubble at the bottom of the Barracca lift, and they joined him briefly. It was obviously legal. At the clifftop, neglected gardens opened into the streets of Valetta, equally rubbled, with sandbagged and boarded shop-fronts, the smell of hot dust, sweatiness, frying onions and dilapidation, but busy with people and loud with noise. Small boys hawked dubious lottery tickets or whispered invitations to meet an obliging sister. Gharries hauled by emaciated ponies mingled with impatient army trucks, and priests picked a way among gangs of labouring soldiers. Windows and market-stalls offered pitifully meagre stocks of fish and vegetables but ample supplies of nylon stockings, church candles and pornographic postcards.

Strait Street was a narrow quarter-mile of pavement that defiled between the drab walls of dozens of tawdry bars, cabarets and cafés, known to generations of blue-jackets as 'the Ghut'. Every doorway vomited discordant music, supplemented by the shouts of a doorman who greeted every approaching group of sailors. 'H'yar, Navy! All your ship's company inside – four stokers an' two marines! Come on, *Daemon*! Chicken an' chips, big eats – best place in Malta!' Inside, there was little to distinguish one establishment from another – shabby seating surrounding a small floor space or a diminutive stage, a dimly lit bar-counter and a drove of women of uncertain age and blatantly painted. In peacetime, Stripey Albright had said, when the Mediterranean Fleet gathered in Malta, women in their hundreds converged on the Ghut from the seaport brothels of France, Italy and Greece, but now there were only the native prostitutes who contorted and baited among the noise and tobacco smoke of the Ghut each night, and at dawn sought absolution in the Church of Our Lady of Victories.

Working for a percentage of drink sales, they received a small metal token with every glass of coloured water purchased for them by patrons, who paid prices that rose steadily as the evening advanced and measures dwindled. Waiters tendered change in saucers with the silver coins covered by coppers, calculating that a fuddled sailor would wave aside what appeared to be only a few pence. Floor shows were perfunctory, usually lewd and greeted with noisy ribaldry. The attendant women winked and wheedled, groped for trouser-flaps, promising – but later, later ...

The evening was young, but in the Wheel of Fortune a handful of seamen were drinking themselves into vociferous incoherence on cheap Marsala. Dancing couples reeled around the floor of the Bing Crosby and the Silver Star, while in the Red Rose a marine, inexplicably naked, pranced behind a shrieking woman who grasped a lanyard knotted to his penis. The Regal vibrated with harsh music that competed unsuccessfully with the adjacent Mae West, where an impatient clientele stamped and shouted for the promised strip show which was being delayed for as long as possible.

'That,' Lobby Ludd winced in the direction of the naked marine, 'is what's bleedin' known as got by the short 'airs.' The Egyptian Queen was quieter, offering only a competition for the Blue Label ale-drinking championship of Malta. A petty officer from *Maidstone* had consumed sixty-six bottles at one sitting and was still in Bighi Hospital. As they sat, two women closed upon them quickly. ''Ello, Jack! I bet you'd like us give you somethin' you've never 'ad before?'

Smithie's eyes widened. 'What 'ave yer got? Leprosy?'

'I'm Marcia,' the second woman told Lobby Ludd. 'I bet you'd like to shag me. I'm French.'

'So's my arse,' Lobby Ludd nodded. 'Shave off.' He eyed her more closely. 'Marcia? Did yer ever know a bloke named Stripey Albright – off the *Veteran*? He mentioned a party called Marcia, at the Gyppo Queen, round about 1926—'

'That's right. I remember,' Smithie said, who didn't. 'She did tricks, like sitting over beer-bottles, an' smoking cigarettes with 'er glut. She could blow smoke-rings.' His interest was aroused. 'Can yer really blow smoke-rings?'

'Not with ticklers,' Lobby Ludd explained. 'They make 'er cough. Only cork-tips.' He signalled a bored waiter to bring two Blue Labels. 'And yer'd better serve the wimmin their crème de menthe, or we'll never get any bleedin' peace.'

'Gin an' Martini, darlin',' Marcia smiled. 'Only two bob a glass.' With the strip show at the Mae West, business in the Egyptian Queen was slow, and customers must be persuaded to stay. She sat closer. 'I've taken a fancy ter you, darlin'.' She stroked his thigh. 'An' Yvonne's taken a fancy ter your friend, ain't you, Yvonne?' Yvonne agreed, and breathed in Smithie's ear.

'I read a bleedin' book once,' Smithie recalled, 'called *Lady, Don't Turn Over*, that started like this, but the next four pages were torn out, and I never did know what soddin' 'appened—' Yvonne had unbuttoned his trouser-flap with the adroitness of long practice. 'But I've got an idea I'm goin' ter find out, any bleedin' minute.' The waiter brought more Blue Labels, two more glasses of unidentifiable green liquid, and then cranked the gramophone.

Yvonne's fingers appraised. 'You want a quick fifty darlin'?' Smithie shook his head. 'I'll spill me beer. Don't yer know anythin' else, like comic songs, or bird whistles?'

'Later on, darlin',' she confided. 'You can shag me, an' your friend can shag Marcia. Then' – she squeezed gently – 'you can shag Marcia, and your friend can shag me.'

'That's what I call a sportin' offer,' Lobby Ludd nodded. 'Yer oughter 'ave season tickets.'

'Two quid each, short time,' Marcia offered, 'or five quid all night in. That includes a Continental breakfast, darlin'.'

Lobby Ludd choked on his beer. 'Breakfas'?' he enquired. 'Shave off. I reckon yer'd need artificial bleedin' respiration.'

The waiter brought more Blue Labels, and Yvonne eyed her empty glass. On another occasion, with the Egyptian Queen filled with tipsy servicemen, she might expect to be moving from table to table, with a drink at each and no lack of obscene proposals. It was the old law of supply and demand, and to a drunk all women were desirable. Tonight, Yvonne could tell, was going to be one of those other nights. She was forty, fleshy, and near the end of her entertaining days, even in the Ghut; only dim lights and heavy cosmetics could hide the ravages of her profession. These were probably her last few weeks in the Egyptian Queen. She might be relegated to a smaller, even sleazier establishment, or pay a small boy to pimp for her, to bring her the spent-out drunks who had missed their liberty-boat. In Malta a woman did not solicit in the streets, but she could do what she wished behind walls, and the priest would absolve her without a qualm.

'If I 'ad a young sister, who's very nice,' Yvonne suggested, 'would you like to meet 'er, darlin'?' She took Smithie's disengaged hand and guided it to the top of her stocking. 'She's twenty.'

Smithie retrieved his hand. 'Roll on. I nearly lost me fingers,' he told Lobby Ludd, and took a fortifying mouthful of beer. 'Did yer say twenty? Where is she?'

'Only in Toni Bajada Lane, darlin',' Yvonne assured him,

'but she won't be finished till midnight. Then you can meet 'er.' She rolled her eyes. 'She's very nice, darlin'.'

'What's she bleedin' doing till midnight?' he asked suspiciously. 'Pullin' stokers' puddings in the Wheel o' Fortune?'

'She's a model, darlin'.' She toyed with her empty glass. 'She always works late, at the Phoenicia 'Otel. Now, you buy me another gin an' Martini, darlin', and tonight you will be *very* 'appy.'

'Well,' Smithie conceded, 'it can't be worse'n Jim Irish's, Lobby.' It was difficult to envisage anything worse than the slovenly doss-houses that offered the only accommodation for all-night libertymen in Valetta. 'All yer can get is a nap hand. There was a bloke, once, who used ter try 'is walking-stick first, jes' ter see if it burned the end orf.'

An incalculable number of Blue Labels later, Lobby Ludd was only hazily aware of his erratic ambulation from the Egyptian Queen to Jim Irish's. Smithie, accompanied by Yvonne, had gone to be introduced to a twenty-year-old model in Toni Bajada Lane who was very nice, although what anyone modelled in a bomb-torn Valetta in 1943 was not entirely clear.

Jim Irish's was a decaying, three-floored house with a narrow entrance-hall lit by a blue lamp that turned faces into corpse-like masks. There was a worn, wooden staircase, a smell of urine and old plaster, and a labyrinth of rooms, each tightly jammed with truckle beds, crumpled mattresses and comatose sailors. The noise of vomiting came from some distant cavern, and someone in the darkness was droning a monotonous dirge that described someone else who was tight as a drum and never been done. A second voice, irate, suggested that, at any moment, the singer was going to have his mouth filled with teeth.

Lobby Ludd eased a drugged leading torpedo-man from his mattress and relieved an equally insensate stoker first class of a blanket. It was highly probable, he knew, that a yet later arrival would do the same to him. He awoke reluctantly in the morning to find Smithie regarding him with red-rimmed eyes.

'Gawdalmighty,' Smithie shuddered. 'What was we drinkin'

last night? Anti-fouling paint?' He groped for a cigarette. 'I've got a mouth like the arse-end of a sewer.' He inhaled smoke painfully.

The room smelled like a brewery.

'My bowels,' Lobby Ludd agreed, 'are what yer might call delicately poised. I daren't cough.' Then he remembered. 'What was yer model like? Shave off. Yer look like yer've 'ad all night in with a vampire.'

Smithie groaned. 'I did. There weren't no soddin' model in Toni Bajada Lane, mate – leastways, not last night. That ol' scrubber Yvonne charged me three quid, *and* four bob extra fer a soddin' French letter.' He shuddered again. 'The worse part was when I saw 'er in the daylight, this mornin'. It was bleedin' cruel, mate.'

'If we can find some coffee,' Lobby Ludd rose carefully, 'that ain't been boiled in the same pot as the onions were fried in—' He was exploring his pockets, frowning. 'Well, I'll go bleedin' sick. I've been robbed – me money and me watch. An' I've lost me cap. Bleedin' Maltese give me the shits. It's a wonder they ain't left me soddin' naked.' He snorted. 'That's what yer get fer giving 'em a bleedin' George Cross.'

four

There had been farewell celebrations in the Bodega and the Taverne Viennois – which had once been the Taverne Anglaise but had discreetly changed its name in 1940 – and the officers' club in St-Nazaire. Braun, Katter and Merker had drunk themselves senseless, and had been carried back to the berth white-faced and sweating. Midshipman Ehlert, inevitably duty officer on this last night, had checked the drunken crewmen as they reeled aboard at midnight. There had been no absentees. Lieutenant Jensen, glassy-eyed, walked with meticulous care to the tiny wardroom, forward, without a word, and Captain Behrmann had been the last. He had stood on the jetty for a long time, smoking a cigar and gazing at the stars, before coming aboard. 'Get to your bunk, lad,' he told Ehlert. 'You'll not have many chances during the next six weeks.'

At dawn, despite the hour, a throng of Wehrmacht bandsmen shivered on the dockside, awaiting U-157's departure, with a film cameraman and two journalists from the Propaganda Ministry, two officers of the flotilla shore staff, a masculine woman in a leather raincoat who presented Behrmann with a small bouquet of damp flowers, and the usual gang of French dock workers. The band exploded as U-157 eased from the jetty, and there were scattered cheers, but in minutes the jetty had disappeared astern, and Behrmann tossed the bouquet over the side, expressionless.

'Wires and fenders stowed, sir,' Jensen reported. 'Hatches secured and guns cleared away. Ready to dive.'

Westward the sky was choked with heavy, dark cloud. Departure from base was an uneasy business. So close inshore there was no possibility of enemy surface vessels, but there was always the danger of a waiting British submarine or, even more likely, of a Sunderland, Catalina or Hudson of Coastal Command, which could pounce out of the clouds without warning. The sea areas immediately adjacent to the Biscay bases were those in which U-boats had to travel, and the British knew it. Thankfully, Coastal Command was the Cinderella arm of the RAF, whose maritime activities were less than enthusiastic and persistently neglected in favour of the more dramatic Bomber and Fighter Command operations. It was odd, Behrmann mused, how short-sighted the British could be in some respects. In March 1943 they had lost 627,000 tons of shipping – a loss which, if continued, must lose them the war – yet they persisted in directing almost the entire weight of their air offensive against targets in Europe, with negligible damage to the German war machine. Didn't the British realize that the destruction of one U-boat leaving St-Nazaire was more vital than several hundred bombs dropped on Germany?

'Diving stations,' Behrmann ordered. 'Clear the bridge. Twenty metres and begin trimming.' The dive alarm-signal hammered, and he flicked away his cigar-stub. 'It's going to rain, so we may as well get below, where it's dry.'

An hour later, in the control room, Behrmann faced Jensen and the Second Lieutenant across the tiny chart-table. 'Our destination is the Caribbean in general and Martinique in particular. It's a soft area – a lot of American shipping, either unarmed merchantmen or USN warships with crews that think the war is something scripted in Hollywood. In Fort de France, Martinique, there has been a Vichy French squadron since 1940, and the American press has been demanding that the French West Indies should be occupied to prevent their being used as supply-bases by our U-boats.' Behrmann chuckled. 'I wish they could, but the French High Commisioner, Admiral Robert, is a stickler for convention, and insists on strict neutrality. The United States Navy is blockading Martinique and Guadeloupe, and their ships are just begging to be attacked. They'll never know what hit them. When we've had our fun off Martinique, we'll move to the Curacao area where there are some oil-storage tanks waiting to be shelled, and after that, gentlemen, there's the Panama Canal.'

Jensen and the Second Lieutenant, Horn, grinned, but Behrmann had not finished. 'We're not alone. Two Type VII U-boats will be leaving Lorient tomorrow to join us, and – would you believe it? – an Italian submarine, the *Bruno*, which somehow got past the Brits at Gibraltar and reached Brest.' He saw Jensen's lip curl. 'Contrary to popular opinion, Italian submarines do not run on olive oil, or fire spaghetti-meatball torpedoes. Undersea warfare is one department in which the Italians are very efficient. We shall give them exactly the same co-operation as we would a German vessel.'

Jensen shrugged. 'Sir – an Italian?' It was preposterous.

'I suggest you reserve judgement, Jensen,' the Captain advised. 'The usual criticism is that the Italians don't do enough. In this case the Italian captain, Cuniberti, was commanding submarines when you were a small boy in knee-pants singing songs about strength through joy.' Jensen flushed, and Behrmann went on. 'Our four craft, with one other, will constitute the Markgraf group.'

Jensen was not to be drawn; he allowed the younger Horn to enquire, 'One other, sir? Another U-boat?'

Behrmann nodded. 'A Type XIV tanker, which will leave Lorient in about two weeks time. We shall rendezvous with her if and when the need arises.' The Type XIV 'Milch Cow' submarine carried sufficient diesel fuel to replenish the tanks of several U-boats, spares and a number of torpedoes. 'It means that, if necessary, we can remain at sea for four months, although I think that's hardly likely.'

'During passage, sir,' Jensen said, 'presumably we shall look for targets.' It was an accusation rather than a question. On the lengthy passage from Kiel to St-Nazaire, Behrmann had shown little desire to sink enemy ships. He had even ignored the British cruiser, and that sort of chance did not often present itself. It was just Jensen's damned luck to have an old-school commanding officer who always had to be correct. Fools like Behrmann should have been purged from the service years ago.

Behrmann nodded. 'An enemy ship sunk anywhere is an enemy ship sunk, Jensen, but we must not lose sight of our objective, the Caribbean. A lot of our people at Befehlshaber der Unterseeboote have put this thing together – including Admiral Doenitz. There are important political and strategic reasons why we should scatter a little mayhem along the American seaboard, and we cannot jeopardize them for the sake of a Brazilian tramp steamer carrying groundnuts to Montevideo.' He paused. 'Excluding the Milch Cow, the Markgraf group will be carrying sixty-two torpedoes, but we're taking them a long way. Any ship we encounter during passage will have to be a worthwhile kill for me to expend resources. We should be off Corunna in about thirty-six hours, and will then run south-south-west to the Cape Verde Islands ...'

The westerly breezes from the Atlantic were cool, almost chilling, as *Susquehanna* swung at her mooring off the west arm of the harbour. She should not tie alongside, FO Gibraltar had decided, and should be under twenty-four-hour surveillance by patrol launches. It was almost inconceivable that any of the prisoners should attempt an escape, but the Spanish frontier was only a few hundred yards away, Algeciras was clearly visible across the bay and the coast of Morocco beyond the Straits. A few hotheads among the Germans might be tempted to do something silly, and there was no point in inviting trouble. Colonel Dunlop, the ship's American comandant, agreed. Invited to dine aboard *Daemon* in company with his second-in-command Major Quinn, the ship's master Captain Pedersen, and the senior Polish officer Major Boleslavski, all four were mildly embarrassed to find the British officers in mess dress and black ties, the table linen spotlessly white, the glass and silver gleaming. 'Don't these guys ever shoot crap or drink beer out of a can?' Quinn whispered, conscious of his own weathered khaki and unbuttoned neck. The British offered gin, repeatedly. Boleslavski had to be helped into the boat at the evening's end, and Quinn had become loudly pro-British.

During exercise periods on deck the German prisoners eyed the summit of the great rock and, more wistfully, the tumble of buildings on the Spanish shoreline. Following several days of adequate food and sleep, albeit in cramped circumstances, many of them had regained a degree of truculence. The ship's broadcast system, tuned to British and American networks, relayed music and news bulletins at which the prisoners jeered. When, on occasions, the song 'Lilli Marlene' was heard, they roared it in German, drowning the loudspeakers, then continued with Wehrmacht marching-songs, stamping their feet. There had been several sullen altercations with the Polish guards, but none serious. On the nearest jetty was a detachment of Royal Marines with Bren guns, and in the harbour were anchored the massive battleship *Nelson*, six destroyers, *Daemon*, *Manxman*, the French cruiser *Georges Leygues*, the depot ship *Maidstone*, and submarines of the 8th Flotilla. There was no doubt that the German consulate in Algeciras knew of the presence of *Susquehanna* and of her human cargo which included twelve generals and more than thirty colonels of the Afrika Korps. It was a frustrating knowledge.

Two days in harbour meant a run ashore for each watch – a single excursion which required to be exploited to the full, and the choice was excruciating. There were the shops and bars of Main Street and Irish Town, swimming in Catalan Bay and from Eastern Beach, or, for the erudite, the Museum, the Trafalgar Cemetery and the Moorish Castle. But, Lobby Ludd told

Smithie, none of these could compare with a bullfight. It wasn't every bleedin' day that a bloke could see a bullfight.

By arrangement with the Spanish authorities and in accordance with international convention, an organized party of naval ratings would be permitted to cross into Spain for a few hours of recreation, for which purpose coaches would be provided. The object of the visit was a bullfight. Names should be given to the Regulating Office by 09.00. Ratings were permitted to change ten pounds into pesetas, officers thirty. Dress for libertymen Number Twos. Coaches would leave the old Tangier Ferry jetty at 13.00. Twenty cigarettes or one ounce of tobacco. No birds, monkeys or other animals were to be purchased ashore. Contraceptives were available from the Sick Bay, one per libertyman. The ship was under sailing orders.

The Master-at-Arms had a jaundiced opinion of Ludd because the latter had returned aboard in Grand Harbour without his cap – having lost it, Ludd said, while leaning forward to help Vice-Admiral Malta into his barge at Customs House Steps, and the Vice-Admiral had told him, Ludd, to tell the Master-at-Arms in *Daemon* that no disciplinary action should be taken. If the Master-at-Arms did not believe it, he could ask the Vice-Admiral. The Master-at-Arms did not believe it, but conceded defeat, promising that he would keep his eye on Ludd henceforth. Lobby Ludd had considered adding that the Vice-Admiral had also recommended a make-and-mend as compensation for his loss, but decided that this might be going too far.

'This time, Ludd,' the Master-at-Arms warned as the libertymen mustered at the midships brow, 'yer'd better not lose yer cap helping Flag Officer Gibraltar orf the coach. An' no birds or animals. Don't come aboard pretending that snakes ain't animals – see? As far as KRs and AIs is concerned, *snakes is animals.*'

The two ramshackle Spanish buses lurched into motion, crossed the airstrip and paused briefly at frontier gates which would have shamed any small-town municipal gardens. Beyond was the dusty stretch of neutral isthmus, then a Spanish policeman, soldiers with Germanic steel helmets and the shabby houses of La Linea. Almost immediately the buses drew into the kerb and halted. They were only four minutes from Gibraltar.

'It's the 'alfway 'ouse,' Lobby Ludd told Smithie, 'like the Fortune o' War when yer go ter Southend.' There was wine, sour Spanish beer, throat-scalding brandy poured from four-star bottles, vendors of tawdry souvenirs, fruit, confectionery, surreptitious offers of allegedly genuine Spanish Fly, smudgily printed copies of *Lady Chatterley's Lover* and equally smudgy photographs of unclothed women that may have shocked Edwardian tourists but inspired little enthusiasm among *Daemon*'s sailors. During the brief journey from Gibraltar, one of the buses had developed an engine defect which was, however, patently a subterfuge of the proprietor to halve his petrol consumption. The sailors clambered into the surviving vehicle, joined by several relatives of the driver.

In a few more minutes the bus shuddered to a halt again. The location, a signboard announced, was San Roque. The sailors alighted thankfully, but there was no bullring in San Roque. There was wine, sour beer and corrosive brandy, Spanish Fly, unexpurgated copies of *Lady Chatterley's Lover*, and smudgy pictures of unclothed, plump *señoritas* in compromising postures. 'This wine,' Lobby Ludd told Smithie, 'is like Parrish's Food. It's got the same bouquet.' Smithie agreed, with similar difficulty. 'A little presumptuous, but with that tantalizing promise o' being bleedin' good fer cleaning brass.' Two stokers were singing a song that required them to stamp on their caps, and the Chief Cook was showing his tattoos to an old lady who only wished to sell him a string-bag of oranges.

The original purpose of the excursion was already becoming blurred and, when the party climbed into the bus for the third time, a number of its members had completely forgotten or no longer cared. The bus had become insufferably warm, crowded with fifty alcohol-reeking sailors, several unidentifiable Spaniards breathing garlic, a woman suckling an infant, bags of oranges, bunches of grapes, and a small grey dog corroded with mange. Smithie took another mouthful of four-star paraffin and winced. 'All me soddin' teeth are loose. Christ knows what it's doin' ter me boots.' He brightened. 'But I've decided what ter be when I get out o' the bleedin' Andrew. Gamekeeper ter Lord Chatterley, mate. It'd be better than bein' the Dame o'

Sark's dog.' Lobby Ludd was unable immediately to see the relevance, so Smithie explained. 'Everyone else on Sark can only 'ave bitches. Think o' that.' Lobby Ludd thought about it.

The third stage of the journey was longer, and at its conclusion the Chief Cook awoke from sleep to find that the small grey dog had been sick over his shoes. Nobody knew the name of the town, and nobody speculated. There were streets with shops and awnings, a few old Fiat taxicabs, kerbside stalls with fruit, water-ices and confections, jostling people and grubby children, dusty shrubs, palms, a hot sun and, at last, a bullring.

It was not the massive amphitheatre that the sailors had visualized but a seedy, wooden stadium leprous with peeling paint, old posters and scrawled graffiti. There were small queues at ticket-windows. 'Ingles! Cojones!' a Spaniard jeered, and raised two fingers. 'Bandidos! Churchill a bastard!'

'An' if yer Aunt Fanny 'ad balls,' shouted a stoker in a mangled cap, 'she'd be yer bleedin' uncle.' The Spaniard, baffled by such logic, was silenced.

With their bottles, oranges and copies of *Lady Chatterley's Lover*, *Daemon*'s sailors seated themselves on crude, wooden planking. In the sanded arena below them a small brass band led a parade of mounted picadors, banderilleros, matadors with capes, and a team of mules. The crowd cheered and the sun grew hotter. The parade dispersed and there followed a lengthy interval during which the crowd became increasingly impatient. Then a bull appeared reluctantly and was goaded into activity by the mounted picadors armed with lances, and harried by long, barbed darts thrown by banderilleros on foot. A resplendent matador strode into mid-arena, whirled a red cape to no apparent purpose, threw away his hat, and finally thrust his sword between the shoulders of the dejected bull. The crowd booed and whistled, and the matador gestured apologetically. The sailors booed, which seemed the right thing to do, and demanded a penalty. The stoker in the mangled cap offered to fight the matador.

The second bull, however, was of different calibre. It came out of its paddock at a thundering gallop, brushed aside a picador's lance, prised horse and rider free of the ground and flung them both, tangling, to the sand. Men ran forward to distract the bull's attention, and he scattered them, but the picador and his horse were hauled to safety. It was the turn of the banderilleros, and within seconds they were running frantically for sanctuary. *Daemon*'s sailors cheered the bull.

But the inevitable was not to be denied. Stuck with festooned darts, salivating, the bull's temper had been sapped. There was a hush as a matador advanced, a roar as he pirouetted, his cape whirling, and thunderous applause as his sword thrust home. The bull fell, defecating, coughing blood.

The corrugated-iron latrine for *hombres* stank acridly and, emerging, Lobby Ludd paused to gulp air. A few yards away, watched by a throng of small boys, a horse lay on the ground with roped feet. A man sat on its head while another, on his knees, thrust spilled entrails back into a six-inch tear in the animal's belly and then sewed up the gash with string. Drenched by a bucket of water, in a few minutes the horse would be whipped into the arena to face another bull.

'Shave off,' Lobby Ludd said, and turned away. 'It's disgusting,' another voice added, from behind him, and it was a voice that was familiar. He did not believe it, but a few feet away, in neat khaki drill, stood Nurse Fiona McCudden.

He swallowed, straightened his cap, and grinned gawkishly, unable immediately to speak. Nurse McCudden's eyes met his, flickered away, and then returned. 'Mr Ludd,' she smiled, surprised. 'What an incredible thing.'

'It's a small world, ain't it?' he contributed, groping for something more intelligent to say. 'It jes' goes ter show.'

Nurse McCudden raised a handkerchief to her lips. 'I'm sorry,' she shivered. 'I must get away from this.' She nodded at the prostrate horse. 'I didn't think I was squeamish, but this—'

She clenched her eyes and, solicitously, Lobby Ludd took her elbow. 'I 'spect there's a first-aid tent,' he suggested, but she shook her head.

'No, I'll be all right, if I can just get out of here. I wish I'd never come.' She suffered his hand on her elbow as they threaded their way out of the stockaded stadium and into the hot street, and he steered her to a small table under the awning of a café. She drew a relieved breath. 'Thank you, Mr Ludd.

I'm not showing a nurse's professional calm, am I? But the whole thing was so horrible.' She smiled wanly, then nodded. 'Yes. I'd love a cool drink, but don't let me be a nuisance. If you're with friends—?'

Lobby Ludd hastened to reassure her that she was not a nuisance and, no, he was not with friends. Well, not exactly. There was nothing, absolutely nothing, that he would rather do at this moment than sit under a shabby awning with Nurse McCudden drinking orange squash. Bullfights were all right, if yer liked that sort o' thing, but when yer'd seen one, he shrugged, yer'd seen 'em all. He supposed that Nurse McCudden didn't come 'ere often?

Nurse McCudden, indignantly, did not. She had come with four other nursing sisters, in two hired cars, from the General Military Hospital in Gibraltar – and, of course, she had forgotten to mention she was now an army nurse. Queen Alexandra's Imperial Military Nursing Service. Lobby Ludd nodded politely, thoughtfully. Would she care for another orange squash?

She declined, looked at her watch and frowned. She really ought to find her colleagues. They had shared two cars, with Spanish drivers, she repeated, but they had not parked in the same place. The car she had travelled in was dark-red, and she remembered a church and a Coca-Cola sign, but it wouldn't matter if they located the other car first. The other car, she thought, had been green, but she did not know where it might be.

Within fifteen minutes they found four churches and thirteen Coca-Cola signs, by which time the streets were thronging with people emerging from the bullring, and the shadows were lengthening. There were carts, buses and cars – even dark-red and green ones – but none that Nurse McCudden recognized.

'You see,' she explained, 'Joan and Beryl might be thinking I'm with Phyllis and Daphne, while Phyllis and Daphne—' Lobby Ludd had already reached the same conclusion.

'Do you think we should go to the police?' she asked. He did not. He entertained no particular animosity towards policemen but preferred to avoid them. Besides, their involvement would mean the end of his own command of the situation.

'You ain't *lost*,' he chuckled. 'I mean, we know where we are.' On reflection, he didn't.

They had regained the vicinity of the bullring and, a hundred yards away, Lobby Ludd could see *Daemon*'s sailors clambering noisily into the Spanish bus that had brought them from Gibraltar, but he rejected immediately the possibility of inviting Nurse McCudden to join the Chief Cook and his tattoos, the stoker with the mangled cap, the bottles, oranges and *Lady Chatterley's Lover*. He reached a decision.

'I'll get a cab,' he said off-handedly.

Nurse McCudden seemed content to place her immediate future in his hands, which was flattering but, at the same time, mildly disconcerting. They found a taxicab with badly worn tyres, a crucifix in the windscreen, and a driver who was unenthusiastic and could speak no English until the question of money was raised. Gibraltar was a long way, he shrugged. He seemed to have no interest in Lobby Ludd's remaining pesetas. It would cost ten pounds *Inglés*, and then only to the Spanish frontier gates; he was not permitted to proceed further.

'It seems a lot of money,' Nurse McCudden said sadly, and Lobby Ludd did not disagree, but he gave a nonchalant laugh and fumbled in his belt.

He might, of course, have left Nurse McCudden in the care of the Spanish driver and rejoined Smithie in the bus; it was the sensible, if not the gallant, thing to do. He debated only momentarily. After all, he was paying ten bleedin' quid.

The rear seat of the cab was less than generous, and he was pleasantly aware of Nurse McCudden's shoulder and thigh pressed warmly against his. The intimacy did not appear to perturb her. He sat very still, not stirring when his leg began to tingle with cramp. He wondered if he might dare to reach for her hand, but decided he dare not.

'I'm more grateful than you can imagine,' she confessed, and gave him a smile that sent his pulses racing. 'I don't know what I would have done if I hadn't met you.' He grunted modestly. 'If you're ever near the Military Hospital,' she went on, 'you really must pay me a call.'

Lobby Ludd glowed with elation. He knew what this was. It was an *understanding*. That's what came of playing the right cards. He wished the cab-ride to Gibraltar could last for hours. And it was a bleedin' good thing he'd saved that ten quid.

They alighted at the Spanish frontier gates and were directed into the guard-house. A Spanish captain smiled at Nurse McCudden and in impeccable English enquired if she had enjoyed her visit. Yes, of course, she was free to proceed immediately. Indeed, he would have a car take her to the British gates. And Signalman Ludd? The captain frowned very slightly. Ah, there were a few formalities which might take a little time. Signalman Ludd had not precisely observed the rules regarding the military personnel of belligerent powers in a neutral country, and the captain would have to make a report. It was a nuisance, but rules were rules. The captain smiled again. He hoped the *señorita* would soon return to Spain; the English nurses were always welcome. He saluted. The *señorita*'s car was waiting.

'I'm sure everything will be all right,' Nurse McCudden assured Lobby Ludd, then added meaningfully, 'When I get back to the hospital, I'll phone the Matron.'

'Please sit down,' the Spanish captain ordered, when Nurse McCudden had departed. He reached for a pen. 'Your full name, rank, number, and ship?'

'Charles Ludd, Signalman, D/JX245613,' Lobby Ludd returned. 'That's all I'm allowed ter tell yer, under the Geneva Convention.'

The captain sighed. 'Signalman Ludd, you are *not* a prisoner of war.' He picked up a sheaf of papers and thumbed through them. 'Ah, yes. Signalman Ludd, HMS *Daemon*. According to this list of names supplied to us by the office of Flag Officer, Gibraltar, you were one of *Daemon*'s party on a recreational visit. Is that correct? Your bus, which was authorized by the Spanish *chargé d'affaires* in Gibraltar, returned twenty minutes ago, but you are still on Spanish territory. You agree? That is a very serious matter, Signalman Ludd. If you are still on Spanish territory twenty-four hours after your entry, you will be interned.' From the wall behind the captain a portrait of General Franco glared at Lobby Ludd accusingly. 'Presumably you are not asking for asylum?' the captain enquired.

'Go an' sit over yer Spanish onions,' Lobby Ludd retorted.

The captain nodded. 'I take that as meaning that you decline.' He continued writing for several minutes in silence, then offered his pen. 'Now, if you will just sign on the bottom line?'

Lobby Ludd stared. 'D'yer think I'm bleedin' *dense*? It's all written in Wop lingo.' He snorted. 'If I signed that, I might find meself servin' ten years in the soddin' Foreign Legion. Shave off.'

The captain drew a deep breath. 'Signalman Ludd, this is merely a statement to the effect that your delayed return to British territory was the result of accidental circumstances, that you have been correctly treated and have not been submitted to any coercion or restraint on the part of the Spanish authorities. It is a routine document which will be filed and forgotten unless you subsequently initiate a complaint. Now, if you will sign, you are at liberty to return to your ship immediately.'

Lobby Ludd considered. 'All right, but I'm warnin' yer. Don't ferget the *Nelson*'s in 'arbour. Bleedin' sixteen-inch guns, mate. Yer won't stand a chance.' He sighed. 'Don't I get a soddin' car?'

At the British gates, to Lobby Ludd's disgust, two uncommunicative military policemen escorted him to a waiting truck and, on the jetty, deposited him with the naval patrol in exchange for a written receipt. A launch conveyed him to *Daemon*'s ladder, and at the head of the ladder waited the Master-at-Arms.

'Ludd,' he smiled blandly. 'I knew it. I knew it from the start. Now yer really 'ave done it. Yer not only adrift with the ship under sailin' orders, yer adrift in a neutral country, provokin' an international incident, arrested by the military, and' – he searched for something else – 'yer need an 'aircut. Yer know what this means, Ludd?' He sucked in his breath. 'It means the glass'ouse. I wouldn't be surprised if yer got sixty days.'

Five minutes later the steel door of the cells crashed shut, and Lobby Ludd, deprived of belt, lanyard, shoelaces and the contents of his pockets, sat on the solitary item of furniture, a bucket. The Master-at-Arms, with grim-set face, strode aft to report to the Commander.

An hour elapsed before the Master-at-Arms reappeared. His face was still grim, but it was also flushed. 'Ludd,' he gritted, 'I don't know 'ow yer do it. The Captain's just come off-shore, where he was dining wi' the General Officer Commanding, see. And they got a bloody phone call, see, from the Matron-in-Charge o' the Military 'Ospital.' He paused. 'The Matron is a very formidable lady. I don't know what she told the Captain, but I know what he's just bloody told me. I got a bollocking. I 'ave to release you from detention, an' there'll be no disciplinary action.' He stabbed a finger. 'I've 'ad my suspicions about you, Ludd, from the first day – see? I don't like your sort. You put a foot wrong, Ludd, and I'll be on top of yer, like a load o' bloody bricks. For a start, get them shoelaces tied!'

U-157 was steering almost due south. For days all radio traffic from *Befehlshaber der Unterseeboote* in Paris had been addressed to the Raubgraf, Stürmer and Dränger U-boat groups to the northward, which were deployed in the path of two enemy convoys, SC-122 and HX-229. There had been nothing for Markgraf, and U-157 had sighted only a few Portuguese boats fishing for hake and pilchards. The northerly wolf-packs were transmitting report after report of ships being sunk, and their total would rise to twenty-one. Lieutenant Jensen was in a foul temper, and the men avoided him in so far as the submarine's confined accommodation permitted.

Surfaced, with the surrounding ocean calm and empty, Jensen and Captain Behrmann were on the bridge when Midshipman Ehlert brought the deciphered signal from the radio cabinet. 'To all U-boats, Atlantic, from Kernéval, sir. Priority intelligence.'

Behrmann grunted, read the signal, frowned, and passed the slip of paper to the First Lieutenant.

'German consulate Algeciras reports departure Gibraltar 10.00 6th April USN transport *Susquehanna* escorted British light cruiser *Daemon* westward bound believed Norfolk, Virginia. *Susquehanna* carrying four thousand Wehrmacht prisoners including senior officers and should not repeat not be attacked.'

Behrmann was thoughtful. 'Ehlert, look up *Susquehanna* in

the Register. I know what a British D-class cruiser looks like – about five thousand tons, twin raked funnels, six six-inch guns.' He had a memory like a steel trap. 'Pretty-looking ships, but not much else.'

Within minutes Ehlert had returned with pencilled notes. '*Susquehanna*, sir – ex-Eagle Steamship and Export Company, passenger-cargo, registered New York, nineteen thousand tons, 530 feet length, twenty knots, oil-fired twin screws, two funnels.'

Behrmann nodded as the photographic image of the American ship took shape in his mind. 'Big, and a good turn of speed. And the Brits don't care if we know. In fact they probably made damned sure our agents got full details, and left it to Paris to order us to keep clear.' He gave a sour chuckle. 'The crafty devils. I can't really think why they bothered with an escort.'

'There's nothing to stop anyone attacking the cruiser,' Jensen said.

'No,' Behrmann calculated, 'but I fancy we're running too far south for the opportunity. Assuming the signal is received by all U-boats, there's really no need for *Susquehanna* to detour, but the Brits provided the cruiser just in case. I suppose there's a remote chance that the transport could be halted by a U-boat and some of the senior prisoners taken off – if she wasn't so fast – but what could the U-boat commander use as a threat? That he'd sink her if she refused to heave to?' He yawned. 'No, Jensen. We'll keep the cruiser in mind, but there's not much we could do about *Susquehanna*. Better to have four thousand of our troops in American prison camps than at the bottom of the Atlantic.'

Three days earlier *Daemon* had taken on oil and fresh water, and on the eve of departure the Paymaster-Lieutenant had presented himself to the Captain's cabin, his cap in the crook of his left arm. Captain Mercer looked up from the small bureau at which he was writing and removed the spectacles that he did not care to be seen wearing.

'Ah, Gasnier.' He frowned. 'There was something I wanted to see you about ...'

'Stores, sir? I have a signal for the dockyard, if you'll approve it. I thought that, if we pass it ashore before departure, it'll save a wireless transmission and a lot of coding up. I've had to anticipate a little.' He looked at a paper in his hand. 'The usual victualling requirements, sir, and rum, medical stores – and we shall need some currency.' Gasnier was a serious young man who felt obliged to explain everything. 'The Engineer Commander has made out a separate requisition, sir – lube-oil, sulphuric acid, electrical cable, cotton waste—'

'That was it,' Mercer said. 'Cotton.' He looked for his pipe. 'You're a Channel Islander, aren't you, Gasnier? Did I hear that you were once a schoolteacher?'

'Yes, sir.' Gasnier was mildly surprised. 'That was before I went into accountancy.'

'What did you teach?'

'Maths, sir.'

Mercer nodded. 'Well, it's not exactly English grammar, but it's the same syllabus.'

Gasnier's face was blank, and the Captain explained.

'The Navigating Officer, Lieutenant Cotton, who is the Communications' Divisional Officer, had a rather outlandish request submitted by one of his ratings, a signalman. Cotton was stymied, so he passed it on to Commander Plummer, who very neatly passed it to me. I make my own rules, so I'm putting it in your lap, Gasnier, where it stays.'

'Yes, sir,' Gasnier said cautiously.

'The rating – Signalman Ludd – has asked for tuition in English grammar. That's right. And he seemed to think that he only had to make a request through the normal service channels for the Navy to produce a schoolmaster like a rabbit out of a hat. Cotton was so taken aback that he mumbled something about seeing what could be done.' Mercer struck another match. 'It seems the rating feels the need to "talk proper", which is an admirable thing, and I don't want the request ignored or treated as a joke. The man's reasons are obviously important to him.' He paused. 'It *might* have something to do with a nursing officer at the General Military Hospital and a dragon of a Matron who had the GOC and me stuttering like schoolboys last night – but I'm damned if I know.'

'No, sir.' Gasnier agreed.

'It's a sort of Pygmalion exercise, Gasnier. See what you can do, will you? Ask around the wardroom – someone may have some books – and, if you're going ashore with that signal, there's a good bookshop in Main Street, near the Piazza. I only hope,' he mused, 'that we haven't started something.'

five

Six hundred miles west of the African coast, twenty-five degrees north, *Daemon,* astern of *Susquehanna,* prepared to turn away. On the TBS ship-to-ship radio-telephone Mercer spoke to Captain Pedersen. '*Bon voyage*, Captain. The met. report gives you good weather for the next few days, and you should have an easy run home. I hope we have the pleasure of your company again at some future time.'

'Thank you, Captain,' Pedersen replied. 'If there's a next time, we'd be delighted to return your hospitality. Quinn wants to find out if your guys can handle Bourbon like they do pink gin, and Boleslavski still swears that someone hit him with a wrench from behind when he came down your ladder. Good luck.'

Daemon turned to starboard, her creaming wake furrowing a mile-wide half-circle in the calm, blue sea that stretched emptily to the horizon. In minutes the two ships were stern to stern with the distance between them widening rapidly until *Susquehanna* faded and disappeared.

Lobby Ludd looked up from the mess-table, where he was chewing the end of a pencil. 'Smithie,' he triumphed, 'I bet yer don't know what a synonym is.' Smithie confessed he did not, but it sounded Jewish. Steevo said it was a French two-door, but it was underpowered and had a sod of a gear-box. 'They ain't made ter be stripped down. Yer've got ter send fer a complete new unit.'

'Around the town the proud brown growler prowls,' Lobby Ludd told them, 'and the same plain Jane came sailing in the rain.'

The passage from Gibraltar, so far, had been uneventful. The weather was warm, and Colonel Dunlop had accepted General Kleinschmidt's request that the prisoners should be allowed the freedom of the upper decks, except for certain prohibited areas, during daylight hours, and as many as possible might sleep on deck at night. The privilege would be permitted so long as discipline was maintained. Boleslavski's guards watched from dozens of vantage-points. Someone had not been very bright, Dunlop considered, putting Poles on this assignment. Boleslavski was a good officer, and he kept his men on a tight rein, but there was an undercurrent of mutual hate that was never far below the surface. Everyone sensed it.

The inherent irritation of ship confinement did not help matters, and Dunlop would be relieved to have the voyage finished with. Disturbances, however, if they arose, were hardly likely to be very serious. *Susquehanna* was a more secure prison than any shore location; if there had been any hopes of escape among the prisoners, they had faded as Gibraltar vanished astern.

Behind them, the Germans in Tunisia were still holding on tenaciously to Cap Bon and the ports of Tunis and Bizerta. Dunlop guessed that there would be unauthorized radios on the accommodation-decks, but he made no attempt to seek them out. The prisoners also listened to the periodic news bulletins on the American Forces Network, and argued among themselves. Some still insisted that the Führer would never abandon North Africa, that there would be massive reinforcements by fleets of towed, giant gliders, that there would be an invasion of Spain. Others insisted that the Afrika Korps would withdraw to Sicily, to man the defences of Fortress Europe, although it was difficult to imagine by what magic carpet a quarter-million men could be transported. Among a growing number there was resignation. In the United States, it was said, prisoners of war had an easy time on farms and lumber camps. The food was good, and there were many Americans of German origin who would be sympathetic. The Americans had never wanted this war with Germany. They had been drawn into it only because of the Japanese ...

Most of them strolled in the sunshine, or sat idly in the shade of the boats, watching the sea that slid easily past, an occasional seabird, the sudden glitter of a flying fish or, astern, the pale-blue British warship that followed in *Susquehanna*'s wake. They watched her until darkness hid her each night, and she was still there each dawn when they awoke, precisely stationed, her radar scanner revolving slowly, ceaselessly. Then, one morning, the cruiser turned her bows away, heeling slightly in the gentle swell, and in twenty minutes was no more than a haze of smoke to the northward. *Susquehanna* ploughed on, alone.

It was just before 4 a.m., still night-cool but threatening to become stickily humid. Ehlert and the Quartermaster made star sightings, and Ehlert went below to make his log-entries. Several crewmen, swollen-eyed, were waiting impatiently to use the latrine, and there was a smell of coffee.

04.00. Morning Watch. Patrol routine. Position 21.50N 27.10W Course 195. Speed 12 knots. Barometer 1010. Wind 2. Sea 2 to 3. Air temp. 70. Sea temp. 74. Cloud 3/8 cirrus. Visibility 8 miles.

On the bridge, Horn had relieved Jensen, and stood with shoulders hunched. To the eastward the sky was pearl-coloured, marred by brush-smears of high cloud, the sea a leaden grey flecked with occasional white. Captain Behrmann climbed from the ladder, filled his lungs with air, glanced at the lookouts forward and aft, at the sky, then raised his binoculars.

'It's going to be a warm day,' he said.

'The news wasn't good this morning, sir,' Horn said. 'The Americans and British have linked up. The British claim to have taken six thousand prisoners in one day.'

'Then they probably have,' Behrmann nodded. 'Was there anything from our own news service?'

'The German–Italian Panzer Army in Tunisia, fighting gloriously against the overwhelming numerical and material superiority of the Allies, has made a strategic withdrawal from the

El Guetta line, inflicting heavy losses on the enemy.'

'That's probably true, too.' Behrmann fumbled in an oilskin pocket for his cheroots. 'The important things about news bulletins aren't what they say, but what they leave out.'

'Sir.' The starboard after lookout cleared his throat cautiously. 'There could be smoke on the starboard quarter.'

Behrmann and Horn swung their glasses immediately. Far distant, at the junction of sea and sky, too low for cloud, was the merest smudge of a shadow.

'It's smoke,' Behrmann confirmed. He waited; then, 'It's a surface vessel – and on almost precisely our own course, overhauling. Increase to eighteen knots.' A minute passed, then two. 'Merchant ship. Alone. Take us down, Horn – twenty metres. Action stations.'

The alarm warning hammered. *'Dive, dive, dive! Open all main vents!'* The bridge cleared as officers and look-outs flung themselves at the ladder, and the hatch crashed home. From aft the roar of the diesels died as the engines were killed and out-clutched, the electric motors engaged, but a compensating roar of air discharged from the main ballast-tanks. The deck tilted. Then, suddenly, there was near-silence.

'Twenty metres. Periscope depth.'

'Thank you. Shut main vents. Trim forward.'

Behrmann spoke from the periscope, and Jensen's and Horn's tense eyes were on his stooped shoulders. 'I have her. Single funnel, two masts, derricks.' He paused. 'Starboard ten – midships – steer two-oh-five.' There was another pause. 'Flood tubes one to four.'

'Tubes one to four flooded, bow-caps shut.'

'Open bow-caps.'

'Tubes one to four bow-caps open. Ready to fire.'

Behrmann straightened. His face was thoughtful. 'A big one. Sixteen – seventeen thousand tons. Over-all drab. About six miles astern on a fine converging course, overhauling. It's going to be so easy, it hardly seems fair.' Jensen and Horn grinned, but Behrmann did not. 'What's the bloody fool doing here?'

Jensen knew what Behrmann was thinking, and shrugged. '*Susquehanna*'s twin-funnelled, sir, and she's got an escort. So it can't be. You said yourself that she wouldn't run this far south.' Jensen was sweating. Vital minutes were slipping by, and this fool was likely to allow a 16,000-ton freighter to slip through his fingers as he had the British cruiser off Ushant.

Behrmann lowered his head again to the rubber mask of the periscope. The closing ship was nearer, but not near enough, in the poor light, to offer anything more than an ungainly profile, almost bows on. With that single funnel, she could be a Liberty Ship; her unrelieved grey paintwork and lack of lights meant she was British or American, and she was steaming at better than eighteen knots. He would have to position U-157 nicely, because after the first salvo there was unlikely to be a second chance. He would allow the freighter to converge to five hundred metres and then turn to bring his bow tubes to bear.

'Stand by tubes one and two. Safety range four hundred.' So easy, it hardly seemed fair.

Lobby Ludd applied himself to the cleaning of the twenty-inch signal-lamp. 'I *shall* clean the lamp. The lamp *should* be clean. The lamp *may* be cleaner—'

'It better be, Ludd,' the Chief Yeoman threatened. 'And, if yer spill any more of that Brasso on the deck, yer *will* be scrubbin' it in the bloody dog watches.'

A few feet away the pneumatic tube from the Main W/T Office suddenly wheezed and the reedy note of the morse intercom sounded urgently. The Chief Yeoman plucked the small rubber cylinder from the tube terminal, extracted the signal it contained, and unfolded it. 'Soddin' arse-'oles,' he grunted, and ran for the bridge.

'Sodding arse-*holes*,' Lobby Ludd said.

On the bridge, Lieutenant-Commander Willis-Paget, Officer of the Watch, swore, and reached for a telephone. 'Captain, sir? Bridge. We've just received a signal on the international distress frequency. *Susquehanna* has been torpedoed. Yes, sir. Her position—' He halted as the telephone spat back at him, then, 'Aye, aye, sir.' He replaced the telephone in its cradle, moved to the voice-pipe. 'Port twenty. Full ahead both.'

Mercer reached the bridge buttoning the front of his shirt. He took the signal from Willis-Paget, read it twice, then thrust it at Lieutenant Cotton, waiting. 'Pilot, I want a course and

ETA, assuming maximum speed – as quick as you like.'

'We're already on course, sir,' Cotton said. 'Two-oh-two. We have roughly twenty hours' steaming. ETA double-oh-three-oh.'

Angrily, the Captain thumbed tobacco into the bowl of his pipe. For the previous sixteen hours *Daemon* and *Susquehanna* had been speeding on opposite courses, the gap between them widening by nearly forty miles every hour.

'This,' the First Lieutenant told Cotton, 'is what is commonly known as an almighty cock-up. Have you still got your seamanship manual? After this, I fancy we'll all find ourselves in Boys' Training.'

'Number One, I want radar and Asdic on their toes,' Mercer ordered, 'and the DC rails and throwers checked.' Thirty depth-charges – enough for five full patterns. U-boats were increasingly operating in packs, a task for hunter-killer groups of destroyers or frigates equipped with H/F Direction Finding, and Hedgehog or Squid forward-throwing weapons; *Daemon* had none of these. His ship's inadequate armament, however, was something that Mercer would think about when the time came. His immediate problem was *Susquehanna*, torpedoed and presumably sinking, twenty hours away, crammed with more than four thousand men. It was a situation that *Daemon* could hardly cope with alone.

'W/T report that both Gibraltar and Freetown have rebroadcast *Susquehanna*'s signal, sir,' the Commander told him, but did not elaborate. They both knew that all ships remotely in *Susquehanna*'s vicinity, circumstances permitting, would be turning towards her last reported position. Meanwhile, it would take Operations a little time to assess resources, formulate orders and cipher them for transmission.

Mercer nodded. 'That U-boat commander couldn't have *known* he was torpedoing a ship full of POWs, could he? You know' – he stared at Plummer – 'I'd have thought that the German naval attaché in Algeciras would have known all about *Susquehanna*, and made damned sure that Paris knew. I could understand a cruiser escort being attacked, but why did they leave us alone and torpedo *Susquehanna*? It doesn't add up.'

'It *did* add up, sir,' Plummer mused. 'One and one made two.

I'll lay five to four that U-boat HQ knew that *Susquehanna* and *Daemon* had left Gibraltar in company within thirty minutes of our clearing harbour. But they couldn't have been certain of our route. I'd say they warned their U-boats, but one of them either didn't get the warning or, when he made a dawn sighting of one unescorted merchantman, he didn't connect her with *Susquehanna*.'

'And he'd need to make a snap decision, in half-light,' the Captain agreed. He could almost sympathize; he knew the feeling – the cold shiver of uncertainty as seconds ticked by, the expectant eyes of others, the flinching awareness that, once in motion, nothing could be reversed. It was the moment of paralysing truth when a man would give his soul to be a thousand miles distant.

The signal, when it came, was brutally concise.

'Daemon *from C-in-C Med repeated Admty, C-in-C Western Approaches, C-in-C South Atlantic, US Chief of Naval Staff Med, FO Gibraltar: Immediate: 070515z = Proceed at utmost speed to position indicated in* Susquehanna'*s 070427z. No other available assistance nearer than Freetown and USN Task Group 17.6 on passage eastward from Bahamas but still thirty hours from you. Intelligence suggests group of four U-boats in Cape Verde area.*'

Lieutenant Cotton whistled softly. 'By the look of that address, we're nobody's baby – a Med Fleet ship positioned nicely between two other commands that don't want us, steaming to assist an American vessel that's just spilled four thousand Germans that we can't accommodate, and there are four U-boats waiting for us to show up. This sort of thing couldn't possibly happen to anyone else, only *Daemon*. There's someone up there, in that big Ops Room in the sky' – he lifted his eyes – 'who's stirring it up for us. We ought to complain to the Fleet Chaplain.'

'That American task group, sir,' Plummer advised, 'comprises the Hornet-class carrier *Peacock*, with Avengers and Hellcats, the cruiser *Anaconda*, and the destroyers *Maddox*, *Bagley* and *Aaron Ward*. Presumably that means some kind of anti-submarine capability.' British opinion of American naval proficiency was low. By early 1942 the Royal Navy had begun to think that the U-boats were beaten, but the entry of the United States into the war had resulted in a savage increase in shipping losses – the larger percentage in waters for which the Americans were responsible. It was easy for the hardened British to blame the Americans' inexperience and infuriating laxity, but there were other reasons – the extension of the war itself, the increase in shipping and, not least, a massive strengthening of the U-boat fleet. Old jealousies, however, died hard; in the Royal Navy's opinion, the American Navy should have stayed in Santa Monica Bay and played with its boats.

Mercer walked to the screen, gazing ahead. *Daemon* had worked up to full speed and her bows were lifting. He would think about the American task group later; they were too remote to give any immediate help. Under normal circumstances a sea-lane like the Cape route would be busy with ships, but the war had reduced traffic to periodic convoys, and there were now vast empty spaces. Mercer wished he knew more. He wished he knew what was happening five hundred miles to the southward. The U-boat commander had not, surely, knowingly torpedoed a ship carrying four thousand of his countrymen? Was he aware, now, of what he had done? What was he doing about it? And, when help arrived in the shape of a British cruiser, how would he and his fellow-commanders react?

'Lock on tubes one and two. Interval five seconds. Bearing oh-four-five. Follow for bearing. Fire when ready.'

Everyone had frozen. It would be a short running-time – only five hundred metres – a muffled detonation, five seconds, then another.

'Tubes one and two fired, sir.'

Behrmann turned from the attack periscope. 'Stand by to surface. Gun-crews to stations.'

There was a deluge of cold brine as the upper hatch slammed open. Behrmann reached the bridge-platform first, followed by Horn, then the 37mm gun-crew, lookouts and machine-gunners. U-157 rolled in a long low swell. Beyond her bows, less than five hundred yards distant, the big, grey-painted merchantman still had way, but had almost slowed to a stop and was listing to port. A plume of white steam vomited from her funnel for a hundred feet skywards, and its screech was clearly audible. They could hear, too, distorted and incomprehensible, a shouting voice from the stricken vessel's address system.

'American,' Behrmann grunted. 'Put a burst behind the bridge, below the aerial feeder, just to discourage the radio officer.' He lifted his glasses. 'Horn, there's a hell of a number of people in that ship.' For several seconds he stared, then his jaw fell. He jerked, whirled. 'Halt Batterie! Jesus Christ Almighty. It's the *Susquehanna*.'

The first torpedo, contact-detonated, struck *Susquehanna* just below her foremast, tore open her thin, welded plating and exploded into the lower accomodation-deck packed with hundreds of prisoners of war. The second, moments later, hit amidships, rupturing two of her six boilers, destroying fuel-pipes and power-generators, and turning the engine-room into a chaos of scalding steam. Main-power lighting failed immediately, but low-voltage emergency power automatically switched into circuit to provide thin but tolerable illumination and keep the telephone system in operation.

There was no telephone response from the engine-room, however. Neither First Officer Jacobs nor his bridge personnel realized immediately that their ship had been torpedoed; they had seen nothing, had heard two muffled rumbles and felt the deck shiver slightly under their feet. For a baffled moment Jacobs thought that *Susquehanna* had hit an underwater obstacle or even scraped bottom, but that was impossible. Then the lights went. Jacobs flashed the engine-room and, failing to achieve an answer, rang the Captain's cabin. His voice was drowned by an ear-splitting screech of escaping steam, and the helmsman was shouting that the ship was not answering to her helm. *Susquehanna* began listening to port, slowing.

Captain Pedersen and Colonel Dunlop, with adjacent cabins, reached the bridge simultaneously, followed shortly by Major Quinn and several of the ship's officers, but Boleslavski, quartered forward, was never to be seen again. There was no doubt, now, about the ship's disablement. Off-watch seamen and engine-room hands were reaching damage-control stations, and reports were coming in. The forward lower accommodation-deck was a shambles, with survivors and guards dragging free the maimed from a tangle of splintered timber, bedding and four feet of swirling water that was still rising. In the meagre emergency lighting, identification was difficult, and Poles and Germans worked desperately together. The engine-room damage was not irreparable, the Chief Engineer reported. Four boilers were still intact, but there was a heavy oil-fuel loss, and it seemed clear that the ship was settling. They would never keep her afloat long enough. In the radio cabin the duty operator switched his transmitter to 500 kc/s, distress frequency.

'CQ CQ CQ de NVXP — RRR RRR RRR ...'

It was only then that someone sighted the surfaced U-boat. She was only a few hundred yards away, to port, but had her bows towards *Susquehanna*, presenting her narrowest profile, and the light was still poor. There were men on her bridge and gun-platform, but she did not open fire and made no attempt to close. A slim, dark hull, U-157 lay low in the sea, rising and falling gently.

'So that's the bastard,' Quinn spat, but there were more urgent matters.

Over the amplified address system First Officer Jacobs was ordering all ranks to lifeboat stations. Several army surgeons, both American and German, were already working over the injured brought from forward, and dressings, splints and morphia ampoules had come from the Sick Bay. There was no panic, but considerable confusion. To a soldier a ship was a foreign environment to which he seldom adapted comfortably, and he was seldom familiar with the maze of passageways and ladders outside those areas which immediately concerned him. It was a transitional phase that he tolerated but of which he was usually glad to be free. In the exceptional circumstances of a torpedoing he was only one of hundreds of disciplined cattle, to be herded as such. The German prisoners had gone to their lifeboat stations, albiet resignedly, every day at 09.00 since leaving Mers-el-Kebir, to be roll-called and then dismissed. It had been easy in the sunshine of day; now nothing seemed the same. The deck was tilting, officers and Polish guards were shouting, seamen were running out hoses, there was a smell of smoke and the lights had failed. Torpedoed? Torpedoed by whom? The Kriegsmarine? A *German* submarine?

'I'll give her ten to fifteen minutes, sir,' the Chief Engineer reported from below, 'and, when she goes, I figure she'll roll to port. If you ask me—'

'Get all your men out, Chief,' Pedersen ordered. He turned to Jacobs, who waited at the address amplifier. 'All injured into the boats. Ship's officers and personnel to abandon-ship stations. Stand by to lower both sides. Release rafts and scrambling-nets.'

General Kleinschmidt, accompanied by a Polish sergeant, had climbed to the bridge.

'I am at your disposal, Captain,' he offered. 'If you will allow me, I will convey any orders you wish to the prisoners of war. The situation is not one that I would have chosen, and I can suggest no reason for the U-boat's action. I have just come from the forward deck, where there are a lot of dead and injured – almost all German. If I can help to prevent any further loss, I would be grateful.'

'Thank you, General,' Pedersen nodded. 'We have only a few minutes. Please instruct all Wehrmacht ranks to proceed immediately to their lifeboat stations if they have not already done so, and to obey all orders given by ship's officers or crewmen. I am about to order the boats away, after which we shall abandon ship. All being well, there should be ample boats, rafts and other floatables to accommodate everyone – if they just keep calm. Tell them to avoid floating oil if they can, and to swim well clear of the ship. When we roll over, we're going to make a helluva big hole in the water.'

Lieutenant Jensen hauled himself from below. 'That ship,' he shouted. 'She's just transmitted a distress signal. Do you know who she is? She's the *Susquehanna*!'

Behrmann choked back his anger. 'I know that. It's a pity you didn't tell me earlier.' But the blame, he knew, was exclusively his own. It had been his decision. 'She's going to go, any moment, so we can't get nearer. I'd say her radio officer was transmitting on emergency power. Tell our operator to retransmit her signal on full power, using her callsign.'

'Are you sure that's wise, sir?' Jensen asked. 'It'll bring every British warship for five hundred miles—'

'Don't argue, Jensen!' Behrmann roared. 'Dammit, just do as you're told!' Immediately, he regretted his loss of calm. Petulance was not going to help. 'When you've done that, I shall have a signal to be coded for BdU.' *Regret I have torpedoed and sunk transport* Susquehanna *square JJ8832. Request instructions.* No – what instructions could U-boat Command possibly give him from the remoteness of Paris? *Am unable to cope with situation alone. Request remainder of Markgraf be ordered to close me at maximum speed.* But even four submarines could do little for four thousand survivors, possibly including many seriously injured. In peacetime, this would involve a massive rescue operation, ships, hospitals, plasma—

Jensen had just regained the bridge when Horn yelled. 'She's going, sir! Christ, she's going!'

The final, awful plunge came sooner than anyone had expected. *Susquehanna*'s decks had been tilting slowly, inch by inch, for minutes, but without warning the tilt accelerated, and five hundred feet of her great, grey hull crashed into the sea, displacing a mountain of angry water that swamped boats already launched and overwhelmed scores of swimming men like ants caught in a mill-race. Several boats, half-lowered or still in their davits, were crushed. The funnel buckled, leaned grotesquely, vomiting choking soot, and a foremast derrick broke free, plunged deckwards to shatter among the hundreds of injured already being flung helplessly over the side, against bulkheads and rails. It seemed certain, for a horrifying moment, that the ship would turn completely over, but she paused as the sea roared into her, the exposed underside of her hull rust-streaked and weed-slimed, her starboard screw still rotating slowly and jerkily against the sky.

Any remaining hope of maintaining order had gone. The jostling queues of men on the boat-deck, many still struggling up crowded ladders, splintered into chaos. The common, all-devouring desire to escape the confines of a doomed ship obliterated all restraint, snapped the last threads of discipline.

Men fought, cursed, tore aside officers, guards and their own NCOs, trampled on fallen comrades to reach the last few feet of deck from which they could throw themselves at a sea in which hundreds already threshed among waterlogged boats, rafts and debris.

Captain Pedersen, Jacobs, General Kleinschmidt and several others climbed from the bridge through a door on the starboard side which, incongruously, opened to the sky. They balanced precariously, treading over portholes and the big porcelain insulators of the radio cabin. The Brooklyn yard had skimped the paint here, Pedersen noted; he'd get the Bos'n's party on it tomorrow. He raised himself, and Jacobs steadied him. 'Don't worry,' Pedersen said. 'I don't hold with captains going down with their ships. Anyway, I'd look damn silly standing on the side of the wheelhouse.' The D/F loop, now horizontal, gave them their last foothold before they took to the water.

'Dead slow ahead, port ten,' Behrmann ordered. 'Break out our life-rafts and inflate the dinghy. Open all hatches. Stand by with a tow-line. Horn – Ehlert – each of you take a couple of men forward and aft. We'll take injured survivors aboard – as many as possible below, then on the casing.' Thank God there was no sea running, and in an hour the sun would be well up. On all sides of U-157 the overladen lifeboats rose and fell, tangling with Carley floats to which men clung desperately, or failed to cling, clawing at floating oildrums, gratings, rope fenders, splintered timber, at each other. There were corpses, like sodden rag dolls with clay-coloured faces, and the sea was thick with oil. Behrmann thought he could count twenty boats, at least two of them under power. He raised his loudhailer. 'Is the ship's captain among you?' he shouted in English, then in German: 'Or the senior Wehrmacht officer?'

A crowded lifeboat bumped against the submarine's pressure hull and a man pulled himself upright. 'I am the senior German officer – Lieutenant-General Baldur Kleinschmidt, late Panzer Gruppe HQ. Presumably this' – he flung his hand in the direction of the sinking *Susquehanna* – 'adds a few thousand tons to your score, Captain, but when you receive your Knight's Cross you'll perhaps not be surprised if the Army does not congratulate you.'

Behrmann saluted. 'Herr General, I am sorry. I ask you to believe that I did not intend this. I believed the ship to be a legitimate target.' He paused. 'But we must mend matters as best we can, sir. I shall take aboard as many injured as possible. Our medical supplies are limited, but we can do something, and I imagine there are doctors among your officers. There are some other matters that I prefer not to shout to you. If you will come aboard, sir, with any other officers you choose, I should like to confer. We may not have much time.'

The General nodded. 'Please ensure that your crewmen do not discriminate between German and enemy injured.' He turned briefly to Captain Pedersen, in the boat beside him. 'You may be assured, Captain, that I shall condone no course of action that is not strictly in accordance with the accepted rules of warfare. If we do not meet again, good luck, and please convey my best wishes to Colonel Dunlop.' Injured survivors were already being lifted into U-157, and other boats and rafts, choked with men, were closing.

'If I were that submarine captain, General,' Pedersen advised, 'I'd have a dozen seamen fending off boats. If he doesn't, he'll be swamped.'

Below deck, Behrmann turned to General Kleinschmidt. 'I have reported the situation to Befehlshaber der Unterseeboote, who in turn have ordered the other three U-boats of my group to proceed to this position at maximum speed. They are U-711, U-759 and the Italian U-boat *Bruno*. I estimate that the first will arrive at about noon, the others within a further three hours. We have received no other orders from U-boat HQ in Paris, which is probably consulting Berlin. There is, however, routine intelligence of an American surface force – a carrier, a cruiser and three destroyers – but it is eight hundred miles to the westward. I am more concerned about the British light cruiser that was escorting you. When did she part company with *Susquehanna*, sir?'

Buckets of hot coffee were being passed up the midships hatch from the tiny galley immediately below it, and sodden, oil-filthy men were being carried forward to the wardroom and petty officers' mess, the torpedo stowage, or laid on the deck-plates anywhere. One, with a leg severed at the knee, screamed obscenities at the brothel-creeping *schweinhund* that had maimed a man who had fought in Poland, France, and from El Alamein to the Kassarine Pass. A hypodermic needle silenced him.

Kleinschmidt frowned. 'The cruiser left us about noon yesterday. I understood she was returning to Gibraltar. She had six large guns, I remember—'

'Six six-inch, four four-inch, twelve torpedo-tubes, and a speed of twenty-nine knots,' Behrmann nodded. 'She would have been steaming northwards at, say, twenty knots, until she received *Susquehanna*'s distress signal, then she would have turned about at full speed.' He calculated. 'I'd say we can expect *Daemon* to join us soon after midnight.'

There was a shout from the bridge. 'The transport's gone under, sir.'

Kleinschmidt heaved an angry breath. 'And what are your immediate intentions, Captain? Out there' – he pointed a finger – 'there are several thousand men, the population of a small town, a lot of whom are going to die unless something is done quickly. There are hundreds of injured who have only hours to live if they don't reach a hospital—'

'Herr General,' Behrmann conceded, 'there is very little we can do until the other boats of Markgraf group reach us. When they arrive, we can perhaps take the boats in tow and try to reach Spanish territory – the Azores or Morocco – from where you can be flown to Spain. The Spanish authorities are usually very obliging in matters of repatriation. However, towing crowded, open boats means a slow speed and consequently a lengthy passage. I don't have to tell you what that means in these conditions. And the British will be hunting for us. We *must* retain our diving capability. I don't know how many passengers a submarine can accommodate without losing stability, but certainly less than two hundred. If we are more concerned with saving lives than with recovering a few prisoners of war, it would be far better to allow the British to pick up the survivors as soon as possible.'

The General glanced around the control room, at the narrow compartments forward and aft, cramped for even a U-boat crew and now with every foot of space occupied by huddled men, chalk-faced or foul with oil, retching, shocked, blood-soaked. And if he climbed to the bridge, he knew, he would see hundreds more.

'There is *absolutely no doubt,*' Kleinschmidt gritted, 'that the British or American ships offer the only hope of survival for a lot of our people, and we cannot make matters more difficult by playing hide and seek.' The rescue of prisoners of war on the high seas would provide wonderful material for Goebbels' ministry and for William Joyce, the radio propagandist, who could ask: 'Where are the prisoners who sailed in the *Susquehanna*?' That a large proportion of them were dead would not be mentioned. Kleinschmidt reached a decision. 'Captain, I believe I am the senior officer here, and I am about to give you an order. You will broadcast a signal to all ships, revealing your position, requesting immediate assistance, and declaring a truce on your part. You will not open fire on any ship or aircraft that does not fire on you, nor interfere in any way with the rescue of survivors.'

six

Knocker White, Telegraphist, brought the news to the mess. 'Yer ain't going ter believe it,' he said, 'but that *Susqehanna*'s been tinfished. As soon as we turned our bleedin' backs. Now we 'ave ter pick the bastards up.'

Steevo paused in the act of peeling a potato, then stabbed at it savagely. 'And I was soddin' watch ashore when we reached Gib. Fer pissing down the sink!' For Steevo, life was one injustice after another. 'Pick 'em up? Why do *we* 'ave ter bleedin' pick 'em up? *We* didn't sink 'em, did we? Roll on my bleedin' twelve.' He pointed his knife angrily. 'I arsk yer. Why should we be deprived of our soddin' rights? We oughter bomb the bastards, mate. *Bomb* 'em. I've a bleedin' good mind ter write ter my MP. After the war' – his eyes narrowed – 'there's going ter be changes – see?'

Lobby Ludd looked up from the mess-table. 'In a complex juxtaposition of situations,' he offered, 'there will inevitably be anomalies.'

'Wot?' Steevo stared.

'My uncle,' explained Jan Prettyman from Bovey Tracey, 'wrote to our MP once, when he were werking fer the Council. Ditches an' gravel. Then he were sacked. "Me 'andsome," he sez, "doant yew never dabble in politics. Yew can't trust they MPs any further than yew'd spread a yard o' muck." '

'There's times,' Steevo decided, 'when I think I'm in a bleedin' mad-'ouse.'

'That ain't all,' Knocker White went on. 'When we get there, there's four U-boats waiting ter knock shit out of us. I've seen the signal. Unless, o' course, we sink them first.'

'Sink four U-boats?' Steevo snorted. 'This clapped-out bucket couldn't sink four bleedin' rubber ducks. I suppose it's Captain Marvel's idea, ain't it? He's got about as much idea as the bleedin' canteen manager.'

'This signal, sir,' the Chief Yeoman told Captain Mercer. 'W/T says it's been broadcast several times, addressed to all stations, on merchant-ship frequency.'

Mercer took the signal, read it first silently and then aloud.

'If any ships can come to the aid of the survivors of Susquehanna *I shall not attack unless I am attacked myself either by ships or aircraft. I have picked up 190 men. Position 21 degrees 40 north, 27 degrees 08 west. A German submarine 07/06.52 GMT.*

'I've never heard of anything like this before.' The Captain frowned. 'Is this joker talking on behalf of all his chums, or just for himself?' He frowned. 'Number One, you've had time in submarines. Can a U-boat dive with 190 passengers?'

Willis-Paget pursed his lips. 'It would depend on the submarine's size, of course, and presumably the commander will know his capabilities, but I'd say he's cutting it fine, sir. And the conditions on board will be sheer bloody murder.'

Mercer nodded. 'Well, he started it.' He raised his cap from his brow. 'I wonder if he would have been quite so concerned over the survivors if they'd been British or American?'

'And even if he's on the level,' Commander Plummer mused, with the signal in his hand, 'this guarantee isn't worth a busted button if other submarines in the area don't fall into line, particularly if U-boat Command has different ideas. Are we expected to refrain from attacking *any* U-boats which may or may not be rescuing survivors? And do we let them *keep* the survivors? They're still the enemy.'

Mercer was thoughtfully silent for several moments; then, 'We're still some hours away, and Admiralty must know the situation by now. If we don't receive orders, I'll break W/T silence and ask for them. In the meantime we will engage any enemy vessel immediately on contact unless she is surfaced, we can plainly see that she is carrying survivors, she makes no hostile or evasive move, and unconditionally surrenders all personnel taken from *Susquehanna.*'

'And if not?'

Mercer shrugged. 'There are too many damned permutations, Joe. Admiralty will have to tell us.'

The Admiralty, it seemed, was also hesitant; the decision expressed in the expected signal took more than an hour to arrive.

'German communication 07/0652 GMT 500 kc/s. You will proceed in accordance with previous orders. Rugby W/T Station now transmitting terms on enemy submarine frequencies to effect that all German vessels engaged in rescue operation will remain surfaced with guns covered and display large Red Cross flag. All repeat all survivors must be transferred to you if practicable or to Task Group 17.6 on its arrival. On completion return to Gibraltar at best speed reporting ETA. Any enemy vessel not complying should be attacked irrespective of circumstances.'

'Well, that's better,' Mercer conceded, 'but it takes a lot for granted. You can bet that U-boat Command are monitoring this signal traffic; I hope our Y-Branch operators are doing the same. It seems to me that all the cards are stacked in favour of the enemy, Joe. They can turn over to us all the survivors in urgent need of medical attention, but there's no way of knowing who they'll have stowed below unless we send boarding parties – and that could mean trouble. That American, Colonel Dunlop, mentioned some high-ranking prisoners, including a lieutenant-general and eleven others – practically all the enemy top brass captured since the African landings.' Mercer shook his head. 'If some of those senior officers have been picked up, I can't believe that the Germans will let a piffling gentleman's agreement stand in the way of getting them back to Germany. I'm not sure that I'd blame them. How would you feel if you had recovered Crocker, Dempsey and Horrocks from enemy hands and were expected tamely to hand them back, when all you had to do was say you didn't have them?'

'There's one way of making sure, sir,' Plummer suggested. 'These orders say, "Any enemy vessel not complying should be attacked irrespective of circumstances." '

Mercer was silent again for a long time. Then he sighed. 'It might have to come to that, Joe. And we'll start something that'll be argued over when the *Lusitania* and the *Athenia* have been forgotten.' He turned. 'Number One, please ensure that the Sick Bay knows what is going to happen. The wardroom and anteroom, officers' cabins, including my day-cabin, and all mess-decks and flats will be cleared, hammocks slung, ready to accommodate survivors. The galley will prepare hot soups and cocoa. Stand by to lower motor-boats and cutters, and release scrambling-nets. All gun-crews will be closed up and searchlights manned. Chief Yeoman, hoist a large Red Cross flag. If you haven't got one, make one.'

'Ludd!' The Chief Yeoman searched for a subordinate. ' 'Ave you used a sewing machine?'

Lobby Ludd considered. 'Not recently, Chief. I utilize the hexpertise of Messrs Bernards of 'Arridge – Harwich – Senior Service Tailors—'

The Chief Yeoman's eyes narrowed. 'Bloody 'ogwash! Ludd, if you think—'

'Interjection,' Lobby Ludd decided. 'That's an interjection, bearing no relationship to the form o' the sentence—'

'LUDD!' the Chief Yeoman roared. 'If you don't get that bloody sewing machine, *at the rush*, I'll interject my boot up your arse, and yer'll bear no relationship to anything yer mother remembered – see?'

By noon, U-157's crewmen had found space for four hundred disabled survivors aboard the submarine, while a further two hundred were in the lifeboats immediately alongside. All forenoon the exhausted soldiers and seamen had been hauled in, given coffee, their clothing dried, injuries tended as adequately as limited stocks of drugs and dressings permitted or, if unhurt, returned to a boat or raft. The crew were already improvising bandages and splints, and the freshwater condenser was working beyond its designed capacity. Steam rose from the open hatches. It was beyond belief that so many human beings could be accommodated within one slim, 240-foot hull and its deck casing; below, the air was stale, thick with the smell of oil, warm metal and antiseptics.

The sun climbed in an empty sky and the temperature rose steadily; neither ship nor aircraft had been sighted. Most of the men in the boats were hardened to the effects of the sun but, somehow, under the circumstances, it seemed hotter than they had known. Among the boats floated corpses, with clothing ballooning obscenely, that refused to drift away.

Only the tiny bridge had been left clear for the vessel's officers, and Behrmann, Jensen and General Kleinschmidt remained there. All three had read the signal, in plain language, that the British had transmitted on low frequency. Kleinschmidt was clearly relieved, but the two naval officers had reservations.

'I can comply, sir,' Behrmann explained, 'but I can't answer for the other U-boats of the Markgraf group. We shall have to wait until they arrive, and confer with their commanders. Even then, we may receive conflicting orders from Befehlshaber der Unterseeboote – who have kept damned quiet. It's my guess that our people are delaying their orders as long as possible, to give the British insufficient time to break the cipher and react accordingly. That could mean that the orders, when we get them, won't coincide with the British idea.' He shook his head doubtfully. 'One thing is certain. We're helpless like this. If there's any damned nonsense, we *must* dive. I shall have no choice.'

The General stared. 'Good God. You don't mean that you'd throw all these men back into the sea, and then fight a battle over them? That's barbaric. Captain—'

'Herr General, this morning I sent the signal you suggested – not because you ordered it but because I agreed. With respect, sir, when it comes to the safety of this vessel and the conduct of any action in which we may be involved, the decision must be mine alone.'

The situation was relieved by Horn, climbing from below. 'A signal from Paris, sir. I've deciphered it.' Behrmann took it, but knew before he had read the two lines of type that the message was too brief to be the one he wanted.

'U-711 attacked by four-engined bomber believed Liberator, suffered damage and ordered to return to Lorient.' Behrmann swore softly.

'That shows how far we can trust the Brits,' Jensen said.

Behrmann grimaced. 'No, it doesn't. The aircraft was probably RAF or American, who haven't heard about the truce arrangement yet. Perhaps U-711 didn't know. It only means that we've lost some of the help we were expecting.' He glanced at the surrounding sea, on which the grey-painted boats and rafts rose and fell under the hot sun, the debris and floating corpses. Soon, he knew, there would be more men dying, then more every hour, and he had not even the means of burying them decently. The sea would be carpeted with floating dead. 'As the British say,' he breathed, 'we're up the creek.'

'RAF Liberator reports surfaced U-boat on southerly course attacked with bombs approximately fifty-five miles north of Susquehanna*'s last position. Hit observed but enemy dived and contact lost. Rugby W/T repeating rescue conditions every hour.'*

'Of course,' Lieutenant Cotton mused, 'we might have expected the bloody RAF to put their big feet in the custard. And even then they couldn't do it right. I sometimes wonder if anyone's told them we're on the same side.'

'And my new paint,' the First Lieutenant gritted, eyeing the blistered and peeling funnels. 'It cost me a bottle of Plymouth to get that duck-egg blue from the dockyard – the last of the peacetime quality, they said, made for Lord Louis. It destroys a man's moral fibre.'

On the flag-deck, Lobby Ludd finished the last hem of the Red Cross flag, and then admired it.

'When you see the Chief Yeoman,' he told Smithie, 'say, "Chief – shave off – whoever made that tiddley Red Cross flag? What artistry! What elegance!"'

'I will,' Smithie promised. 'So yer'd better get it 'oisted before he sees it too close. If yer 'adn't told me, mate, I'd 'ave thought it was Japanese.'

Lobby Ludd stood back a few feet. 'To the critical eye,' he confessed, 'it might lack symmetry.'

'No, it ain't that,' Smithie said. 'Yer could see it a mile off. There ain't nothing like it in the Fleet Signal Book. I mean, if we always knew what every bleedin' flag was, there'd never be any surprises in life.'

When Captain Mercer came to the bridge in the early afternoon he glanced at sea and sky, then thumbed through the sheaf of intercepted wireless signals that had accumulated during the previous hour. 'Radar?' he enquired. 'Captain. Anything to report?'

'Radar to bridge. Nothing to report, sir. Searching.' The voice was mildly hurt.

Mercer lifted himself into his chair. *Daemon* thrust through the placid sea, throwing aside a churning bow-wave and tumbling smoke from her hot funnels. It would have been like this, Mercer mused, on that humiliating February night, the previous year, when the light cruiser had flung herself out of the darkness of Southampton Water into the Solent. *Scharnhorst* and *Gneisenau* were in the Channel and, even though the odds against *Daemon* were suicidal, her torpedoes might get home and the German ships at least be delayed sufficiently for heavier British forces to concentrate. At utmost speed, the Admiralty had demanded, and *Daemon* had obeyed – but her navigator, anxious to save minutes, had miscalculated, had ploughed his ship's bows into Calshot Sands. Had the manoeuvre been successful, it would have been hailed as brilliantly daring; but it had failed, and the court martial, convened aboard Nelson's old *Victory* in Portsmouth, had reached a verdict of negligence without a dissenting vote.

But that had been someone else, Mercer assured himself. Now he had followed his orders exactly, and there was no possibility of *Daemon* running aground here. There were two thousand fathoms under her – enough sea to hide every submarine in the German Kriegsmarine. He knew there were four somewhere.

He frowned. 'Y'know, Joe, the enemy's keeping damned quiet. It's been nine hours since *Susquehanna* was sunk, more than six since the U-boat asked for assistance, and five hours since Rugby began transmitting the rescue conditions. But, so far as we know, there's been no response.' He fumbled for his pipe. 'You'd think there'd be a squeak from someone, wouldn't you?'

'And you'd think that aircraft had never been invented,' Plummer added. 'Perhaps they're deliberately keeping clear of the area after this morning's business, but a reconnaisance report would be very useful.'

Mercer was not listening. 'The trouble is,' he said slowly, 'we always think in English, and they think in German. The result's not necessarily the same.' He drew a pensive breath. 'Three or four U-boats, beyond reach of any material help. A torpedoed ship, three or four thousand survivors, mostly German and a lot of them injured. Those U-boats haven't a hope in hell of getting more than a handful of them back to Germany. Even if, by some miracle, they managed to get those survivors to Spanish, Portuguese or Vichy French territory, they'd be interned.'

Plummer nodded. 'So they might as well be left to us. The Germans can't win.'

'Yes, they can, Joe. There's *Daemon*, and there's a 20,000-ton carrier, a cruiser and three destroyers, all about to congregate like flies around a jam-pot. The U-boats will have fifty-odd torpedoes between them. They can take aboard all the top brass from among the survivors, and leave the rest swimming. Then, all they do is dive, and wait for us and the Americans to arrive, flying our pretty Red Cross flags, and begin lowering boats.'

He chuckled grimly. 'It'd be like kicking bottles off a wall.'

'No.' Plummer shook his head. 'No, sir. They wouldn't dare. They could never live it down.'

'They'd dare all right, Joe. They'd dare. And since when did the Germans ever worry about living things down?'

The sewing machine reminded him of the suit.

It had been a beautiful suit, Lobby Ludd recalled wistfully – a masterpiece in blue serge – and he had worn it only once. There would probably never be another like it, and now it rotted at the bottom of the North Sea with his hand-sewn collars – not forgetting his white silk scarf and Burberry.

He had arrived in RNB, on that first occasion, straight from Boys' Training, and realized within the hour that there were two kinds of sailor; those who were content with the ready-made, ill-cut uniforms issued by the Navy and conforming rigidly with Admiralty Instructions, and the others, more discriminating, who achieved a higher sartorial level by having their uniforms made to measure by a naval tailor. He was, albeit without choice, one of the first category.

From whatever source the naval rating obtained his uniform replacements, he was required to buy them; there was no gratis issue after the first one on enlistment, but his pay was supplemented by a small sum – Kit Upkeep Allowance. This, however, was less than adequate for its intended purpose, and most sailors arranged a credit account, maintained by monthly payments, with one of a number of well-established naval tailors with branches in most ports.

'As soon as you've signed the allotment form,' the assistant told him pleasantly, offering a pen, 'I'll measure you for a suit. Ten shillings a month? A pound? I think you're very wise. Anywhere in the world. Yes, you just write; we have your measurements. Anything. Clothes, shoes, watches, gifts, flowers.' There were branches in Gibraltar and Malta, an agent in Scapa Flow. 'On the dotted line,' the man said, 'and your official number. That's it.' He reached for a tape measure. It was a wonderful idea, Lobby Ludd agreed. He didn't understand why nobody had thought of it before.

'Best Canadian serge, of course,' the man nodded. It could

not be anything else. 'And the neck down to about here?' He indicated Lobby Ludd's navel. 'Cuffs lined with blue satin. Inside leg? And bottoms – shall we say twenty-eight inches? Gold badges, of course.

'Ah, yes. You'll need a cap – one of our silk-lined range – and shoes. John White's Superior black calf. And collars. Med-blue, with hand-sewn tapes. Cap-ribbon, gold wire – and a new black silk.' He hummed speculatively. 'Now, you really ought to have a Burberry. We have our own line, excellent quality, guaranteed.' It was impossible to imagine being without a Burberry, and the mere thought was anathema. 'A white silk scarf? Of course. And you haven't got a watch ...'

It had been a beautiful suit. When unwrapped, it glowed with the sheen of newness. It fitted with absolute perfection, hugging his hips, and the twenty-eight-inch bell-bottoms fell smoothly over his immaculate black-calf shoes. The neck was deeply slashed, trimmed with long, swallow-tailed ribbons, the cuffs were snugly buttoned. If the Prince of Wales had served on the lower deck, he would have worn a suit like this. Lobby Ludd refolded it carefully, inside out, the trousers in their five horizontal 'concertina' creases. It was too good for Union Street. It was a suit for the Hammersmith Palais, or King's Road, Chelsea. He might wear it in Liverpool, where the destroyer *Virtue* only waited for Ordinary Signalman Ludd to join her, and where a man could swagger with his silk-lined cap on the back of his head, his cuffs turned casually back to reveal blue satin linings.

'I don't think I've finished payin' them off yet,' he told Smithie, 'and I only wore it once. In Liverpool, in the black-out. Then we went ashore in Polyarnoe in duffel-coats and seaboots, an' on the way back there was this tinfish. Sper-lash.' He sighed. 'Except the watch. That was shock-proof and water-proof, until I slept at Jim Irish's. Then it was just missing.'

The Chief Yeoman had appeared. He glanced upward, then froze. 'What,' he snarled, 'is *that*?'

'Ah, yes, Chief,' Smithie remembered. 'Shave off. 'Oo did make that tiddley Red Cross flag? What artistry! What bleedin' elegance!'

*

U-759 and *Bruno* achieved the rendezvous within twenty minutes of each other – the German, a Type VIIC of 769 tons surfaced, lead-grey and severely functional, the larger Italian painted a rich blue, with an impressive escutcheon fixed to its conning-tower. Both vessels eased alongside U-157 and secured. 'Please have your crews continue attending to injured,' Behrmann shouted. 'I should like to confer with both captains aboard *Bruno*, but I must first get away a signal to BdU, confirming your arrival and requesting further orders.' Five minutes later he faced his brother commanders in the tiny wardroom of the Italian submarine.

They shook hands. 'I am delighted to see you, gentlemen,' Behrmann said. 'I wish the circumstances were different.' Oddly, he had met Commander Vincenzo Cuniberti several years before, during a visit to the Italian base at La Spezia, but was unacquainted with his own countryman, *Oberleutnant* Loerzer. He outlined briefly the events of the previous few hours, watching them. Cuniberti, a man of his own years, met his gaze, nodding. Loerzer's eyes were lowered, his mouth sullen. Another Jensen, Behrmann decided.

When he had finished, Cuniberti shrugged. 'A great pity, Captain, but it could have happened to any of us. The important thing, now, is what we can best do towards saving the most lives.' He paused. 'For many of the survivors there may not be much time.'

'And you, Loerzer?' Behrmann asked.

Loerzer grimaced. 'The Markgraf group has already lost U-711, probably because she was on the surface to achieve maximum speed in reaching this rendezvous, but there are still three of us. I suggest that as soon as we sight an approaching vessel – which will probably be the British cruiser – we proceed on passage in accordance with the original orders.'

'That will mean putting hundreds of the worst injured back into the boats, which are already crowded to capacity,' Behrmann frowned. 'It would take several hours, unless we simply threw them over the side, and that's not to be thought of. There have been five or six amputations since dawn. There are broken limbs and three Americans badly burned, at least one lung perforation and a skull fracture – if it matters, a major-general.

Scores of men have swallowed oil. And I'm only talking about the men on my ship and immediately alongside. God knows what's in some of the boats and rafts. There are several doctors working with lifeboat first-aid kits. No' – he shook his head – 'if we do as you say, Loerzer, it would be the finish for hundreds of these men who might otherwise be saved. I see no alternative but to wait openly for the British cruiser to arrive. She is not a big ship, but she will have a surgeon, trained medical attendants and a sick bay. Then we must wait for the American task group.'

Loerzer was reluctant. 'Very well,' he nodded, 'but, in that case, I don't think we should come out of this empty-handed. You say you have General Kleinschmidt aboard U-157, that there were twelve generals and thirty Wehrmacht colonels in *Susquehanna*—'

Cuniberti interrupted. 'Lieutenant, before you say what I think you're going to say, I must make my position clear. The British cruiser will be here in about ten hours, the Americans some time tomorrow. I firmly believe we should wait for them, in the meantime doing all we can for the survivors. However, if you both insist, I am prepared to make a run for the nearest neutral port – but not just to return a handful of your generals to Germany. It will be for all the survivors, or none of them. It means either Tenerife in one direction or Dakar in the other – both about eight hundred miles. Towing the boats, at a rough guess, it will take us eleven or twelve days. I don't know how we shall feed them, but perhaps that does not matter. Of course a lot of them will die from their injuries, or exposure – perhaps a thousand – but they are not Italians, so they are not my concern. And, of course, we may not cover fifty miles before the enemy air search finds us. However, if that is what you decide to do, I will co-operate. What I cannot do is offer an exclusive passage back to Berlin for senior officers.'

'With respect, Commander—' Loerzer burst out, but checked himself. The curtain of the small cabin had been drawn aside, to reveal Lieutenant Jensen. He held a slip of paper in his hand, and there was smug satisfaction in his face.

'Sir' – he addressed Behrmann – 'an action-immediate signal from BdU, for decipherment by officer only. I took the liberty.'

He grinned. 'I think this answers all our problems.'

Behrmann read the signal in a flat voice, his face expressionless.

'Request for assistance has been passed to French Government in Vichy through Armistice Commission. French Navy is despatching one cruiser, two sloops and one gunboat from Dakar and Konakry to your position at utmost speed. British terms for rescue operation are not accepted. You will revert to war deployment immediately and endeavour to intercept and destroy British and American warships now closing you, but first take aboard all senior Wehrmacht survivors you are able to accommodate. On completion of operation return St-Nazaire.'

seven

To the Chaplain's resentment, the small Chapel of St Peter in *Daemon* was too frequently utilized in other roles, as the venue for the ship's modest lending library, a quiet sanctuary for letter-writing, a meeting-place for the canteen committee and, more recently, for Paymaster-Lieutenant Gasnier and Signalman Ludd. The Chaplain had tentatively complained to the Captain, but had been politely rebuffed. Space in any warship with a wartime complement was at a premium. The ship's company's church service, when circumstances permitted, was held on the quarterdeck, and a weekly Communion service for a half-dozen faithful did not justify an exclusive appropriation for religious purposes. Regretfully, the Lord's occupancy must be shared.

Lieutenant Gasnier had not embarked upon his task with enthusiasm, but neither had he expected the assignment to be either prolonged or arduous. Ratings got odd ideas occasionally, Lieutenant Cotton assured him, like becoming Seventh Day Adventists, studying Yoga, or building a ten-foot model of the Taj Mahal with matchsticks, but their dedication did not long resist the conflicting distractions of the Fleet Club or the Egyptian Queen. He had known a rating once who had a pair of eyes tattoed on his buttocks accompanied by the words 'I see you'. It just went to show. Lieutenant Gasnier was not sure what it showed, but he spent a whole evening polishing up his own grasp of the essentials of grammar and syntax, just in case his pupil showed more determination than Cotton suggested.

Signalman Ludd, however, was more than just determined. He had armed himself with a signal pad, three pencils, a ruler and an eraser, and began devouring nouns, verbs and conjunctions with such voracity that, startled, Gasnier was himself thrown back on the necessity for daily study to meet the requirements of each coming session. English grammar was not his subject, he told an unsympathetic Lieutenant Cotton. 'Why doesn't the fellow want to knit socks, or collect beer-bottle labels, or mess about with glue? Why does he have to be a B.Litt? He's one of yours, isn't he? Why don't *you* turn in every night muttering, "Tommy will ring the bell, Tommy rang the bell, the bell has been rung"? I mean, it's a bit thick, old boy. It's affecting my whole way of life.'

'You're doing a grand job, Gassy,' Cotton explained. 'Who knows what uncut gem you have in your warm little hands? This chap Ludd could be First Lord one day. A. V. Alexander was a stoker, wasn't he? That's what I mean. Little acorns and all that. If you play your cards well, Gassy, you might end up as Under-Secretary.'

Lieutenant Gasnier was not placated but, to his relief, his dog-watch obligations were suddenly halted. The chapel's seating had disappeared, to be replaced by a table covered by a brown rubber sheet, an anaesthetics machine, cylinders, a trolley of instruments, mounds of linen and dressings, a smell of disinfectant and a sick bay petty officer.

'That's a pity,' Lieutenant Gasnier said.

Lobby Ludd nodded. 'Yessir. It looks like we'll have to use your cabin. I don't mind.'

'It don't look like that at all, Ludd,' Gasnier said firmly.

'*Does* not, sir,' Lobby Ludd suggested. 'The pronoun "it" is singular, therefore "it" *does* not look like that at all. If you remember, sir, "Old King Cole *was* a merry old soul", not "*were* a merry old soul"—'

'Oh my God,' Gasnier shuddered.

The pseudo-Gothic Church of St Barnabas in Wimbledon was gauntly ugly, cold, and smelling of withered flowers and the small paraffin stove immediately under the pulpit, with a sparse congregation comprised largely of old ladies and a cohort of Wolf Cubs. Under normal circumstances Lobby Ludd would not have remotely considered going to church, but it was a small price to pay for the other. Now that things had happened the way they had, Freda Harris explained, with the inference that they might happen again, he ought to show that he had more than just that in mind. He thought he understood what she meant.

'Charlie,' she said slowly. 'On Tuesday night, when it happened – you know—'

He nodded. 'When yer got the 'ang of it, yer were ten-guinea. What yer need is practice.'

'What I mean is – when you came to—' She hesitated. 'I mean – were you *careful*? Afterwards, I had a horrible feeling—'

He had experienced the same feeling himself, but he snorted. 'There's blokes that do it fer years, and never ring the bell.' It would be just his luck. 'I'll show yer ternight. It's the old people's whist, ain't it? I'm *always* careful—'

'Always?' she bridled. 'You mean you do it with others? Not with Eileen Wilkins? I couldn't *bear* it.'

'O' course not,' he scoffed. 'Eileen Wilkins? Shave off. Yer don't think I fancy *Eileen Wilkins*, do yer?' He did fancy Eileen Wilkins but, when he had unbuttoned his trouser-flap against the static water-tank, that young lady had indignantly refused to co-operate. 'It ain't that. It's instinct, see. You wait till ternight, an' I'll show yer what I mean. If yer go through life,' he philosophized, 'worryin' about being in the spud line every time someone shags yer, yer might as well be in a convent.'

Freda agreed, doubtfully, that she supposed she might, but her doubts were revived later when, with the Reverend and Mrs

Harris absent and hopefully long detained, she had submitted to Lobby Ludd's vigorous demonstration on the settee. She squealed suddenly. 'Charlie!'

He had assumed the ejaculation to be an expression of ecstatic approval and, encouraged, he redoubled his efforts; he always knew he had a natural flair. Freda, however, struggled to a sitting position, her eyes wide. 'Charlie!' she gasped. 'Did you—? I'm sure I *felt* something! Are you sure you didn't—?'

'O' *course* yer felt something,' he retorted. 'Yer *supposed* ter feel something. What do yer think I'm doin'? Physical jerks? No, I ain't done nothing. I ain't come to it—'

Freda was unconvinced. 'Not even a little bit? It only takes a little bit.' She was studying animal genetics at the Fulham Polytechnic. 'With artificial insemination it's diluted and put in a fridge, and one boar can serve dozens of sows. You'd be surprised how many.'

He groaned. 'Gawdalmighty.'

'It's not that I want to be a spoilsport,' she apologized, 'and I know what happens when men suppress their sexual desires. They get terrible headaches.' She considered. 'Well, if you're really sure, Charlie . . .' She lay back and closed her eyes, waited expectantly, then opened them again. 'Oh dear,' she sympathized. 'It didn't stay up long, did it? Was it something I said?' She glanced at the clock. Lobby Ludd drew a deep breath. 'There's a book in the library,' she recalled, 'by Dr Marie Stopes. I'll look it up. Perhaps you're not getting enough red meat.'

Mr Harris's entrance was predictable. He unwound his long woollen scarf, switched down the electric fire, then beamed at Lobby Ludd. 'Good evening, young man. Have we met before?' Lobby reminded him that they had met only three nights earlier. 'Of course,' Mr Harris agreed. 'You were shot down. I know *exactly* how you feel. Exactly.' He peered at the clock. The Harris family, Lobby Ludd decided, had an obsession about clocks. 'But you must have coffee before you go, dear boy. You really ought to come earlier. Freda, dear, you must bring your young man earlier. It's unkind to keep him up this late.' He had a sudden thought. 'You must bring him to St Barnabas.'

*

She steered him to a pew. 'Charlie,' she whispered, 'do you know what today is?' He thought it might be early-closing day, but she squeezed his arm. 'It's St Valentine's Day. It's the only day in the year on which women can propose to men.' Fortunately, the congregation had risen to sing 'All hail, the power of Jesus' name!' He cleared his throat purposefully.

'Charlie,' Freda persisted. 'You do love me, don't you?'

Lobby Ludd sighed. 'O' course I love yer. I shag yer, don't I?' If you want to know what a party will look like in twenty years, Bungy Williams had once said, take a look at her mother. Mrs Harris was a small, shapeless and birdlike lady who wore lisle stockings, sensible shoes, and dentures, and always smelled faintly of Lifebuoy soap.

'That's not the same thing,' she said, then allowed the passage of a further verse before resuming. 'Charlie, you must have a talk with Father. On Sunday. I'll tell him you're coming to lunch on Sunday.'

Lobby Ludd nodded. On Sunday he would be in RNB Devonport, waiting for a draft chit.

'Of course,' she breathed, 'it must be at St Barnabas.'

'Hello,' Commander Plummer observed. 'Down in the forest something stirred. Things are hotting up, sir.'

'*Admiralty to* Daemon. *Reliable intelligence indicates Vichy French cruiser* Gloire *and gunboat* Annamite *departed Dakar and sloops* Bougainville *and* Dumont d'Urville *departed Konakry at short notice approximately 1700z/07. Course and speed uncertain but no apparent reason other than* Susquehanna *sinking.* Bullfinch *ordered from Bathurst to contact and shadow. All efforts must be made to prevent enemy recovering high-ranking prisoners using any means at your discretion. Avoid confrontation with French warships.*'

'That's about as easy as having a haircut in a revolving door,' Plummer said.

'*Bullfinch*?' Mercer frowned. 'What's that?'

Lieutenant Cotton had checked. 'Coastal minelayer, sir – 498 tons, speed ten knots, crew of twenty-four. Armament twelve mines, one Oerlikon, two Lewis guns.'

'I think we can forget all about *Bullfinch*,' Mercer decided, 'and I doubt if there'll be any confrontation with the Frenchmen. Both we and the Americans will have reached *Susquehanna*'s last position long before anything can come up from Dakar. But the French aren't coming because of any regard for us, Joe. We haven't been their favourite navy since we bulldozed their fleet three years ago. No, they've been ordered out by Vichy, at Berlin's request.'

'And that means the U-boats in the area can forget any responsibility towards the injured survivors,' Plummer added. 'You could be right, sir. The trouble is that we won't know for sure until we get a tinfish up our kilt.'

'Have the hands gone to supper?' Mercer asked. 'We'll go to action stations at twenty-two hundred. It's going to be a long night.'

There had been a heated exchange in the tiny wardroom of *Bruno*. However distasteful the orders were, Loerzer insisted, they were orders, and Befehlshaber der Unterseeboote must have balanced the consequences. The destruction of the British cruiser and then the American task group, and the recovery of two or three dozen senior Afrika Korps officers from enemy captivity would be a *coup* that outweighed any question of ethics and was surely worth the loss of a few other survivors who could never regain Germany anyway. Commander Cuniberti said that Befehlshaber der Unterseeboote could go to hell. The circumstances had changed but the rules of the game had not; it was a matter of complete indifference to him whether several thousand lives were saved by the French or the Anglo-American ships, or both, but one thing was certain – he would not use those lives as a decoy.

Behrmann wanted to agree with Cuniberti, but Loerzer's argument was unassailable. What were ethics in total war? Had there been anything ethical about the bombing of defenceless Rotterdam, the crushing of the Poles, the invasion of Russia, the concentration camps and the gas chambers? What had been ethical about Italy's attack on France or, for that matter, the British action against the French fleet in 1940, the American Lend-Lease activities, the Japanese attack on Pearl Harbor? In any case, Behrmann could not compel Loerzer to disobey the orders from BdU. Whatever Behrmann said, Loerzer could make his own decision. Both, ultimately, must answer to the U-boat supreme commander, Admiral Doenitz, and, with near-certainty, to the Führer.

'I agree with Lieutenant Loerzer,' he said slowly, 'but you, Commander' – he did not lift his eyes to the Italian's face – 'must do as you wish. I will begin immediately to discharge all my injured into the boats, then U-157 and U-759 will take aboard as many officers as is possible without impairing our fighting efficiency.'

Cuniberti shrugged, not hiding his disgust. 'In that case, gentlemen, I would like to be under way as soon as possible, towing as many boats as I can manage.' He glanced at a chronometer on the bulkhead. 'I doubt if my speed will exceed four or five knots, but I will head southwards, for Dakar, which means that I shall either meet the French squadron or be overhauled by the British and Americans if – as I hope – you fail. Now, if you will please rejoin your own ships, I have a great deal to do.'

The scene from *Bruno*'s upper deck was horrifying. More debris, released by the sunken *Susquehanna*, had reached the oil-clogged surface – more corpses, bedding, sodden kitbags and tangled clothing. For a mile surrounding the three submarines, moored together, the sea was dotted with lifeboats and rafts, crammed with men and low in the water, rising and falling with every swell. From the nearer boats men were shouting at the U-boats' crewmen, anxious to be taken aboard, but Loerzer had seamen on both forward and after casings, fending off. *Bruno*, sandwiched between the two German vessels, had cast off her lines, and Cuniberti eased her slowly ahead.

An incredulous General Kleinschmidt confronted Behrmann. 'Your First Lieutenant has just told me something I cannot believe. Are you seriously intending to abandon all these men – even off-load the injured you have on board – in order to destroy the very ships that *you have asked* to save them? Are you mad?' For answer, Behrmann thrust BdU's last signal into the General's hand, then turned away. 'Jensen,' he ordered, 'you know what is required.'

*

Cuniberti had got away first with eight boats chosen indiscriminately and carrying 300 men, turning to southward and slowly increasing power until he achieved his maximum speed compatible with safety. He intended to heave to every hour to replenish the boats' water supplies, to distribute coffee. *Bruno*'s 37mm gun was covered by a tarpaulin, and a six-foot Red Cross flag was draped around the fore of the conning-tower. Three hundred men represented only a token percentage of the several thousand from *Susquehanna*; Cuniberti dared not take more, but with him on the submarine's bridge-platform stood Captain Pedersen, in Italian overalls and rope-soled shoes.

'There is heavy cloud coming up from the south,' Cuniberti noted. It was beginning to dusk. 'There will be no moon.'

Pedersen made no comment. He did not understand what was happening and he did not wish to fraternize with his captor. Presumably there was a purpose in the submarine's southerly course, but he could not guess it. At this slow speed they could not make a landfall for days, and below deck were three of Pedersen's men who were going to be dead if they did not soon reach a hospital or a ship's sick bay. He did not understand why the German submarine, U-157, had begun to lift injured survivors back into the boats from which they had earlier been taken, unless the arrival of rescue ships was imminent – in which case, why was the Italian towing eight boats away?

'I am sorry, my English is not good,' Cuniberti said. He smiled. 'You know something, Captain? I was born in New York, in Hoboken. You know Hoboken? But I left before I was one year. If my parents had remained, I might have been in the American Navy.'

Pedersen grunted. 'And I was born in Sweden. If my parents hadn't emigrated to Minneapolis, I'd still be a goddamn neutral.'

It was not until the forward torpedo compartment, the most inaccessible, had been cleared of all survivors that Behrmann could order his two expended bow tubes to be reloaded, and it was a lengthy, exhausting task. The deck-boards had to be taken up, the stowed, grease-smeared torpedoes hoisted by chain-tackle, their contact pistols checked, and then each inched carefully into the waiting orifice of an empty tube. By the time Chief Engineer Braun reported the reloading completed, the sky was darkening.

Evacuating the crowded survivors from within the U-boat and lifting the disabled through the three narrow hatches was even more laborious and distasteful. The crewmen blasphemed. It was incomprehensible that men with fractures, burns, even the unconscious, must be disembarked to make room for officers who themselves were baffled by the exchange. They argued, and some refused. There was angry shouting, and several boats pushed away. In the deepening gloom it was almost impossible to distinguish between oil-filthy, dishevelled officers and equally grimy troops and seamen. There was blood and stained dressings on the deck-plates, five dead, and a wrapping of human fragments that Petty Officer Mohr thrust into the disposal chute, choking. On U-759, Loerzer was experiencing similar difficulty. A dozen angry soldiers had clambered on to his after casing, refusing to return to their boat even when he manned his machine-gun, and obeying only when he threatened to dive. The dinghies and rafts of both U-boats had been pressed into service, and a group of Poles on a float that clung persistently to U-759's stern sang scurrilous songs and jeered loudly at every German discomfiture.

Darkness had closed before the U-boats got under way, and the sky had clouded heavily; the darkness was intense. The British cruiser, Behrmann had estimated, would reach the vicinity at any time after midnight, approaching from northward, but there was an uncertainty factor of several hours. It might well be nearer dawn. Both captains would remain surfaced unless or until submersion was absolutely essential. They needed to conserve battery power, while the submarines were so crowded that, submerged, conditions would become intolerable in a very short time.

Daemon would have Asdic and probably radar, Behrmann calculated, and a modest number of depth-charges, but radar had not been very successful in the detection of surfaced submarines with an above-water profile of only a few feet. The U-boats could afford to remain surfaced, at least during darkness in which, in any case, a periscope sighting would be difficult if not impossible. Neither Behrmann nor Loerzer wished to wait until the cruiser had stopped to pick up survivors. The enemy would be helpless, but the consequences could be horrific. *Daemon* must be intercepted.

The American task group of five warships was the unpredictable element of the operation. Its whereabouts had been only vaguely defined in a routine intelligence signal, and it could be days or only hours away. Logically, it should approach from the west or north-west, but the carrier-borne aircraft could cover 300 miles in an hour and explode from the clouds at any moment. The only prerequisite was daylight.

A pale shadow against the blackness of sea and sky, *Daemon* pounded southwards, all lights darkened. Her bow wave rose phosphorescently, streamed, sparkling, along her flanks and tumbled astern, to die as the funnels' smoke sank over it. The long hull vibrated and boiler-fans drank air with an unceasing roar. Below, mess-decks and passageways had been switched to dull red lighting in which men stumbled about their duties, and nobody slept. In the director station, high above and abaft the bridge, the Gunnery Officer had tested communications. Closed up with him was the director-crew – range taker, rate officer, director layer and director trainer – awaiting the order to load all guns, which would energize the 'gun-ready' lamps. Torpedomen were gathered in the waist, talking in low voices, and aluminium buckets of cocoa were coming up from the galley. All guns were cleared for action, and the depth-charge party waited in the tiller flat. On B gun, someone was playing a mouth-organ softly.

In strategic positions, damage-control groups checked hoses and hydrants, foam guns, timber and bolts of fearnought. The chapel was now an operating-theatre, and there were casualty stations in the sick bay and the officers' bathroom flat. Paymaster-Lieutenant Gasnier stood at the plot-table, below the bridge, watching Cotton pencilling his final calculation. Cotton glanced up, grinned. 'If I've done my sums right, Gassy ...' He moved to the bridge voice-pipe.

On the bridge, Captain Mercer nodded. 'Thank you, Pilot.'

He was silent for several moments; then, 'Number One, reduce to half-speed, please. We don't want to run anything down.' *Daemon* was twenty-five miles from *Susquehanna*'s last position.

'Radar to bridge. Surface echo, bearing three-four-five, about ten miles and closing, speed twelve knots or less.'

'What does it look like, Joyce?'

There was a pause of twenty seconds. 'Small, sir. It could be a string of lifeboats with radar reflectors, but I'd say not—'

'Not at twelve knots,' Plummer muttered.

'About the weight of a drifter or ML, sir.' Joyce hesitated. 'Bearing now three-four-oh. It could be a surfaced submarine.'

Mercer rested his eyes thoughtfully on the Commander. There was not much time. 'I wonder if he knows about centimetric radar?' he mused. 'All right, Number One. Bring us round to a converging course, please. I want the target fine on the port bow. Director, all guns load CPBC. Stand by depth-charges, please. Pattern of four, rails only, minimum setting. Searchlights, make ready.'

'All guns, load, load, load.'

'Asdic to bridge. Target dead ahead, seven miles and closing.'

Daemon's six guns, all mounted on her centre line, were not turreted. Their crews wore anti-flash clothing and were otherwise protected only by a gun-shield of one-inch steel. They worked with incredible speed, to a drilled pattern from which every unnecessary movement had been eliminated. Each breech snapped open, projectile and charge rammed home from the loading-tray, the breeches slammed. Already the next shell and charge were waiting. In the director and the transmitting station below – where the Admiralty Fire Control Table computed range, course, speed and muzzle velocity – the 'gun-ready' lamps glowed red.

'All guns loaded, ready to fire.'

Eyes strained ahead, and a minute dragged past, but the night was impenetrable beyond a few hundred yards. 'Radar, how's it looking?'

'Radar to bridge. No change, sir. Target still on course, dead ahead, about five miles and closing.'

'Reduce to ten knots,' Mercer ordered. If it was a U-boat, its commander obviously considered himself safe from visual, Asdic and radar detection. He was right on the first two counts, but not the third. German submarine intelligence did not yet know of a recent British scientific breakthrough – the resonant cavity magnetron – which allowed radar to fasten with certainty on distant objects as small as a U-boat's conning-tower. With a little luck, and the noise of her engine-fans reduced, *Daemon* could glide through the darkness, her claws bared, to within a half-mile of an unsuspecting enemy.

On the other hand, the U-boat was capable of launching a salvo of four torpedoes from her bow tubes in almost as few seconds, which would destroy *Daemon* before she could fire a shot.

'Ah, good morning, young man,' Mr Harris had beamed. It was Sunday. 'Don't tell me. You were shot down. I know exactly how you feel. If it helps—'

'Torpedoed, Daddy,' Freda corrected. 'This is Charlie. He's a signalman in the Navy. *You* know.' She looked at her father meaningfully. 'You were going to have a talk.'

Mr Harris frowned blankly, then remembered. 'Of course.'

'I'll help Mummy with the lunch,' Freda said, and smiled at Lobby Ludd over her shoulder.

Mr Harris folded his hands in his lap and cleared his throat. 'It's all so difficult in wartime. Our Mr Wignall was excellent, but he went into the Pay Corps, and Miss Purdey has never really managed, especially with the wig-wagging. She never really mastered wig-wagging.'

'Wig-wagging?'

'They have to do it for their signalling badge,' Mr Harris explained. 'The Scouts, you know. Miss Purdey had the Cubs until Mr Wignall left us, but now she has the Scouts. It's very difficult, especially with the weekend camps. Some of them are fourteen.'

'I see,' Lobby Ludd nodded. He didn't.

'I always have said that, if you can't send your son to a good school, you can at least put him into the Scouts.' Mr Harris examined his stubby fingers. 'Of course, we don't have the tents in the open. We put them up in the church hall. Well, Miss Purdey is a lady of mature years, but with boys of fourteen it's a *little* awkward.'

Lobby Ludd nodded again.

'Naturally, I was delighted when Freda told me about you, Charlie. I'd do it myself, but I have to sleep on a special mattress. Now, every Scout has to bring one food item, like baked beans, tinned tomatoes, corned beef, herrings in tomato sauce, and that sort of thing. It's tremendous fun. They have games and a sing-song. I expect you know lots of sea shanties. And then they all have cocoa before turning in.'

Lobby Ludd's eyes narrowed.

'Sometimes I do a recitation – usually Kipling. Do you know any Kipling? "Kamal is out with twenty men to raise the Border-side, And he has lifted the Colonel's mare that is the Colonel's pride . . ." '

'I don't know that one,' Lobby Ludd said, 'but I know some others.'

'Splendid.' Mr Harris was enthusiastic. 'You know, you ought to drop into the church hall this evening. Why don't you meet me there about eight? Miss Purdey would be delighted. Perhaps you could show the Scouts some knots. Better still – artificial respiration. That's always a little awkward for Miss Purdey.'

When Freda reappeared, Lobby Ludd was drinking a glass of sherry. She glanced coyly at him, then at her father. 'Have you—?'

'It's all settled, my dear,' Mr Harris beamed, with his rear to the electric fire and bouncing gently on his toes. 'It's a most happy arrangement, and I couldn't think of a better choice. We shall start the ball rolling immediately – this week.'

Freda squealed ecstatically. 'This week? But aren't there lots of things to do – like announcements, and catering? What will Mummy say?'

Mr Harris shrugged benevolently. 'I don't see why your mother should be involved. I'll make the announcement in the usual way, with the Sunday School notes and the old people's whist. As for catering, I've already explained to Charlie that everyone brings one item, and their own plate, cup, knife and fork.' He placed a warm hand on Lobby Ludd's shoulder. 'Charlie's agreed to come to the church hall this evening, and we're going to run through the procedure with Miss Purdey. There are just one or two things he ought to know, and Miss Purdey has been doing it for months.'

'Miss Purdey?' Freda was bewildered. 'What's it got to do with Miss Purdey? If it's going to be a rehearsal, shouldn't I be there?'

Mr Harris was equally surprised. 'I really never thought you would be interested, my dear. You never have been before. But of course you may come – we'll go together. As for Miss Purdey – well, I'm sure both she and Charlie can learn something from each other. He can show her his knots, which are sailor's knots, and probably quite different from any she's seen before. She can decide if they're suitable. If there's time, they can wig-wag. She's always had to do it from a book, and it's not the same as having someone like Charlie, who's doing it all the time.' He looked at the clock and then patted Lobby Ludd's shoulder again. 'Well, how about lunch, dear boy ...?' He wandered out.

Freda was incredulous. 'Did he only have one sherry, Charlie? I've never heard him say such things. He must have suppressed it for years, poor man. And Miss Purdey! To look at her, you'd never dream she was like that. She must be at least forty.' She squeezed his arm anxiously. 'If you get there first, don't you do anything until I get there.'

'Well, if yer like,' Lobby Ludd agreed. He did not understand any of it. 'I could give a recitation.'

'That's it,' she said. 'Give a recitation. I think Daddy must have had some of the home-made parsnip. He drank some at Christmas and trod on his glasses.'

The Reverend and Mrs Harris, accompanied by Freda, arrived at the church hall shortly after eight o'clock. Mr Harris had already been surprised by his daughter's sudden interest in the Scouts, but the insistence of the usually meek Mrs Harris on joining them was incomprehensible. She and Freda had whispered in the kitchen, and Mrs Harris had determinedly pinned on her hat. It was an occasion, she told her husband firmly, on which any mother would want to be present. Mr Harris protested that, while the acquisition of Charlie Ludd was gratifying, surely it wasn't *that* important? It could probably all be left to Miss Purdey. At that point Mrs Harris had drawn herself up to her full sixty-one inches. That creature, she observed icily, should never be left alone in the company of young boys. It was disgusting. To Mr Harris it was also baffling.

Just inside the black-out curtain, Miss Purdey sat on a chair twisting her handkerchief. She was flushed. At the opposite end of the hall Lobby Ludd stood under the totem pole surrounded by seated Scouts, who listened to him rapturously. He was reciting.

Mr Harris beamed. 'Splendid,' he whispered. 'Is it Kipling?'

Miss Purdey drew a deep breath. 'The first one was called "Eskimo Nell", then "The Good Ship Venus". Now he's started again.'

'Excellent,' Mr Harris chuckled. He turned to listen.

'There's a dirty male urinal to the north of Waterloo.
There's another one for women lower down.
There's a girl named Alice Brewer,
For a shilling you can screw her,
Or sleep with her all night for half a crown ...'

eight

There were two forward lookouts, standing back to back at the bridge-screen and peering ahead and to beam. The distant end of the jumping wire that stretched 110 feet from bridge to bows was lost in the darkness, but they could see the green glitter of the sea as it broke away on either side, and the lines of the planking over the forward casing, where the 88mm gun-crew huddled. The diesel engines throbbed, swelling throatily when the outboard exhausts lifted clear of the water, then diminishing when the vents were awash. The after lookouts stood at the hand-rails above the 37mm gun-platform, watching the black void beyond the vaguely discernible pale gleam of the wake.

Occasional crewmen had come from below, to breathe clean air for a few minutes and then return to the stale below-decks, where control-room ratings, artificers, electricians and torpedo-men worked at duty stations that were cramped under normal circumstances and were now impossibly crowded with fatigued Wehrmacht officers who slumped everywhere, some apprehensive, others numbly resigned. In the tiny hydrophone cabinet the operator sat hunched with his headphones hung from his neck; his equipment was useless against the noise of the diesels.

It was Jensen's bridge watch from midnight, but Behrmann remained with him. The Captain was painfully tired. He had been on his feet for twenty hours, since *Susquehanna* had been sighted, and that seemed weeks ago. Extreme tiredness sapped a man's resolve. He wished he had never seen *Susquehanna.* He wished he had been anywhere else. *'U-boote Heraus!'* the propaganda posters in Bremen had shouted. 'U-boats go forth!' The U-boat commander with the grimly chiselled features, drawn by some ministry artist who had never been to sea, stared from the poster with confident eyes that never needed sleep, never ached with fatigue, never searched empty horizons for endless hours. Britain was being starved to death, the Führer assured the German people, and Admiral Doenitz promised new devices – the acoustic torpedo and the Schnorkel breathing facility – which would finally tip the balance in the see-sawing war at sea. Even at this moment the U-boat packs in the northern Atlantic were winning; the enemy tonnage being destroyed was higher than ever before. But, Behrmann suspected, it could not last. With the North African campaign almost finished, the enemy could now direct his full attention towards the Atlantic, with escort carriers and the increasing numbers of hunter-killer destroyers and frigates, new anti-submarine weapons. It would take more than acoustic homing torpedoes to enable the U-boats to hold the ring. It required flesh and sinew, dedication and endurance. Behrmann knew why his veteran crewmen, Braun, Katter and Merker, drank themselves insensible at every shore-going opportunity.

Guiltily, Behrmann wrenched his thoughts to the present. That was the hell of being so damned tired. A man's awareness became blunted; he began to withdraw into an inner self that was like a cocoon. He lifted his face and sniffed the air. The wind that had brought this heavy cloud was from the southward – the south-east trades. It was a pity. The distinctive smell of funnel smoke could carry for miles at sea, but not against an adverse wind. 'I think,' he said to Jensen, 'we'll stop engines for a hydrophone sweep—'

His words were torn away by Jensen's frantic shout, 'Ship ahead! Ship dead ahead!' – then the screech from a forward lookout, *'Feindlicher kreuzer in sicht!'*

The next instant they were blinded by the merciless glare of a searchlight. The alarm klaxon screamed. *'Dive, dive, dive!'* It was going to be too late, Behrmann knew. The four look-outs had flung themselves down the bridge hatch quicker than they had ever done in practice. 'Clear the gun!' Behrmann shouted, but Jensen, leaning over the rail, was also shouting at the 88 mm gun-crew below. 'Fire, damn you! Fire!'

It had been hardly believable that the target on the radar screen could continue on course, as indifferently unaware of its peril as a minnow that swam blissfully into the waiting jaws of a monster pike. In a few more moments the jaws would snap shut.

'Gunnery radar on target, sir. Red oh-oh-five, nine hundred yards . . .'

Nine hundred?

'If we get much nearer, sir, we'll be too close for main armament.'

On the bridge nobody moved or spoke. Mercer stood on splayed legs, head thrust forward. Aft, the depth-charge party crouched at the rails. Every gun that could bear was precisely ranged and tracking, the 'gun-ready' lamps glowed, the Gunnery Officer waited for the order and the Director Layer's finger was on the fire trigger. Mercer thrust back the two words that fought to climb into his throat. He had to be absolutely certain. He had to be sure that the vessel in the blackness ahead was not a fishing-boat or a small freighter in waters where it should not be. Whatever it was, enemy or otherwise, its captain was going to be the most shocked man in the entire Atlantic in just ten seconds.

'Increase to half-speed,' he ordered. He waited for the Coxswain to acknowledge; then, 'Searchlight.'

'The noblest of things,' Lieutenant Cotton murmured, 'are sweetness and light.'

The broad pencil of brilliant blue leaped from the searchlight platform, stabbed at the darkness beyond the bows, moved fractionally left, and then fastened cruelly on the small, humped shape, a mere quarter-mile distant, a white plaster toy on a sea of jet of which every tiny detail was distinctly visible – conning-tower, periscopes and aerial, deck-guns, rails. Along the thin flanks were exploding feathers of spray as ballast-tanks were flooding in a desperate attempt to crash dive, but it was going to be too late.

'Slow engines,' Mercer snapped. 'We'll ram.' But not bows on, at speed. He had seen what had happened to the destroyer *Hesperus* as the result of a similar attack – her bottom ripped out for a quarter of her length and three months in dry dock. *Daemon*'s momentum was more than sufficient to take her into the U-boat with crushing force. 'Ready with depth-charges?' If the submarine survived the cruiser's 5000 tons, then a few hundredweight of high explosives would finish her.

Nobody would believe it if they hadn't seen, Lobby Ludd would tell and retell later. It was the silence of it, with the white whale of the U-boat speared by the searchlight and blowing frenziedly as *Daemon* bore down – not fast, but almost leisurely, and with the certainty of death. Nobody shouted, but all simply watched, awe-struck.

Then, with the sea already breaking over U-157's foredeck, the totally unexpected happened. There was a crash of a gun, a sudden, explosive flare that shocked all watching eyes on *Daemon*'s bridge and flag-deck and, overhead, an echoing, massive thunderclap that had everyone crouched and flinching. Uncomprehending, Lobby Ludd found himself on hands and knees as severed halyards, aerials and splintering glass insulators deluged around him, and there was smoke in his throat. He clawed himself upright and immediately stumbled over the

Chief Yeoman, who swore. 'We've been bloody hit.' The next moment the ship shuddered as her bows met the submarine, bit obliquely but deeply, ploughed on, shearing the thin, welded plates of the enemy's port tanks from their ribs, from fore-plane to midships, with the ease of a fish-gutter's knife. Lobby Ludd and the Chief Yeoman, both dazed and involuntarily clutching at each other, stared as the U-boat rolled, slowly, then suddenly, exposing her gangrenous underbelly and open flooding-flaps. She was still rolling like a water-sodden log as the sea closed over her, and *Daemon* shook free.

'Full ahead, fire pattern!'

The depth-charges ran off the stern rails in pairs, two, four, six, eight, in rapid succession as the cruiser's wake boiled. There was a pause, and then the sea opened with a murderous roar that shivered every rivet in the ship's stern. A mountain of white water climbed high, hung for seconds, and collapsed slowly in a welter of spray that was lost in the darkness as *Daemon* forged ahead. No hull ever built could have lived in that cataclysm, far less a submarine already broken, capsized, and with half her ballast-tanks destroyed.

Within the U-boat all was indescribable, hopeless chaos. Men were flung against bulkheads and machinery; they clung to handwheels, were torn loose, clawed for life, at controls, motor-casings, at each other, as the submarine rolled and continued to roll. There was a screech of tearing steel that tortured the ears, and the hull shuddered madly. Behrmann, smashed against the bridge-ladder and with blood filling his eyes, fought back the nausea of concussion. Could a submarine turn completely over and survive? 'Blow all tanks!' he shouted. 'Full pressure!' But his voice was a croak. He heard Braun say something, and then there was a monstrous, shattering explosion that obliterated everything. 'Fore-planes not answering,' Braun said calmly. 'Anyway, she's going. We can't hold her.'

The lights failed and there was utter darkness. Men sobbed. If only, Behrmann thought, he had never sighted *Susquehanna*. If only he had not attacked. If only he had listened to Cuniberti. If only he had stopped engines for a hydrophone sweep ten minutes earlier.

'One-ninety metres,' Braun said. 'Two hundred. Two ten—'
Only another seven thousand to go. His eardrums had gone, and he was deaf.

Lobby Ludd pushed open the door of the Bridge Wireless Office, which automatically switched off the interior light, and Steevo, who was peering angrily into the opened top of his B28 receiver, dropped his tobacco into his lime juice. 'Shut the bleedin' door, will yer?' he fumed. 'Anyone would think this is soddin' Paddington Station. There's blokes coming in, then goin' out, then coming in – an' now I've lost reception. All I've got on this bleedin' thing is fresh air.' He regarded his sodden tobacco morosely. 'Jes' look at that. 'Ow can anyone smoke that? If it was kye, it wouldn't be so bad, but bleedin' lime juice!' He shuddered. 'What was all that soddin' panic about?' He stared at Lobby Ludd. 'Did someone fill yer in?'

'We rammed it – the U-boat,' Lobby Ludd said, 'but she got off one shell from her deck-gun. It must have been aimed at the bridge, but it went high, smashed the radar lantern and the starboard yard, and brought down half the aerials – on top of the Chief and me—'

'Shave off,' Steevo marvelled. 'No wonder I can't 'ear bugger all. I've got no soddin' aerial.'

Lobby Ludd sat in Steevo's vacated chair, shaken. 'Haven't you got any lime juice without tickler in it?' Steevo searched for the jug. 'I wouldn't be surprised,' Lobby Ludd speculated, 'if there weren't a few medals.' He fancied a medal. He wondered what Nurse McCudden would think, if he had a medal.

'Medals!' Steevo scoffed. 'Soddin' arse-'oles. If this bleedin' ship can sink a submarine, there'll be kids knocking 'em down with sticks next.' He shook his head. 'Jes' look at that tickler. It's bleedin' ruined.'

The First Lieutenant made a damage report. 'No apparent hull damage forward, sir, but we're still waiting to hear from the Engineer. The enemy shell must have missed the flag-deck by inches, torn away the upper ladder without exploding, and been deflected upwards to burst against the radar lantern and bring down the lower yard. Radar's completely destroyed, and W/T says the aerials are a shambles, but they can make do, and they'll rig juries as soon as it's light.'

'Casualties?'

'None desperate, sir, but they're all signals personnel – two yeomen and a signalman on the flag-deck and two signalmen in the SDO – concussion, cuts, broken ribs. The Chief's all right, and he still has three ratings.'

The Captain nodded. 'Thank you. It's a damned nuisance, but we can live without radar. It could have been worse.'

It was worse. The Engineer Lieutenant-Commander telephoned the bridge. 'There's a godalmighty vibration on the port shaft, sir, and I'd like to take an inspection party into the tunnel immediately – and I mean right away, sir. Can we stop engines? The port screw may have fouled the submarine's pressure hull and been wrenched out of true, or it could have been that shallow depth-charge pattern—'

Mercer swore, spoke over his shoulder. 'Stop engines,' he ordered, then returned to the telephone. 'How long will it take? This is a nasty place to be a sitting duck.'

'Twenty minutes, sir – half an hour. I'll make it as quick as I can. But we've got a very expensive noise down here, sir, and whether it's the shaft or the screw we're not going to fix it with glue and string. I'd say we'll be reduced to single screw until we can dock.'

The Captain replaced the telephone in its cradle. 'Number One, order all non-essential machinery and power generators to be stopped. I want the ship quiet. If that U-boat had any running-mates, they won't be far away – and they'll be listening.'

U-759 was listening, several miles to westward, surfaced and stopped. Reciprocating engines, the hydrophone operator reported, very faint but closing, bearing oh-two-five. He watched the bearing widen very slowly. A surface vessel, at a guess moving north to south. Range? Not less than five miles, but still closing. Twin-shaft geared turbines. Yes, only one vessel.

Oberleutnant Loerzer deliberated. Whatever the vessel was, it was steaming into Behrmann's sector. He, Loerzer, would listen and wait until either the hydrophone operator reported the muffled, underwater noise of an explosion or, after a calculated interval, it was clear that the unseen vessel had not been intercepted by U-175. In the latter case, Loerzer would follow discreetly. The ship was not going very far – only as far as the abandoned boats and rafts of *Susquehanna.*

The operator's reports were relayed to the bridge-deck. *'Oh-five-oh, closing. Oh-seven-oh, constant. Oh-eight-oh, constant ...'*

The night was as dark as pitch, and Loerzer could see nothing to eastward; visibility was less than a mile. *'Oh-nine-oh, constant.'* Due east and passing. He would wait a little longer. Twin screws and alone. It must be the British cruiser. The opportunity for destroying a cruiser did not present itself often, but he would allow Behrmann first throw. Loerzer raised his glasses; they were useless. A cruiser would mean an iron cross with oak leaves, perhaps a visit to Berchtesgaden, but Loerzer would happily concede the cruiser in exchange for the American task group. It would put him high on the list of U-boat aces – Prien, Schepke, Kretschmer and Loerzer ...

It happened as he half-hoped it would not. *'Explosions, sir! Precisely on bearing.'* Loerzer and the bridge lookouts whirled, scanning eastwards, but the blackness was absolute. 'That was a rumble, sir,' one of the lookouts said, and a second agreed, but Loerzer was not sure; at times like this men heard what they wanted to hear. 'A lot of distant turbulance, sir,' the hydrophone operator resumed. 'It could be a vessel breaking up – bulkheads going.' The trained ears of the operator were more reliable.

A minute passed, then another. 'Hydrophone—?'

'Nothing, sir. Propeller noises have ceased. I'll keep sweeping.'

Loerzer peered at the luminous dial of his watch. In two hours it would begin to lighten and a new day of uncertainty would begin. He would listen for another ten minutes, then take the submarine south-westwards. He needed sleep to clear the thickening fog of fatigue from his thinking, and by the forenoon there might be a position and course report on the American task group. If, in ten minutes, there were still no propeller noises, he could assume that Behrmann had sent the

British cruiser to the bottom. It was a deep bottom, he mused – the fringe of the Cape Verde Basin, 14,000 feet. Probably a sinking ship never did reach bottom, but drifted, suspended in limbo, a mile or so down, for ever.

The Engineer Lieutenant-Commander reported in fifteen minutes. The port shaft was sound. It was the screw, perhaps the bracket. As soon as the ship docked, they could have a diver down to determine the nature of the damage, which might be rectified by underwater repair in days. To work the port engine to destruction could mean a dry dock for weeks, if they ever reached a dry dock. And he would recommend a maximum of 200 revs on the single screw unless an emergency arose . . .

Mercer nodded, frowning. 'Thank you. Pilot, a course, please. We can't be more than spitting distance from *Susquehanna*'s boats, if they haven't scattered – twenty miles, if Pedersen's position was anything like accurate. In a couple of hours we'll be getting some light. All right' – he put a cold pipe into his mouth – 'let's get the old lady under way. What are we complaining about? We've just sunk a U-boat, haven't we?'

'If the damage is serious,' said Smithie, who hoped it was, 'it's got ter be a dry-dock job, see. And they won't dry-dock us in Gib, mate – it'll have to be Pompey or Guzz.' Fortune was smiling on *Daemon* at last. 'Think o' that. There's got ter be seven days each watch, then engine trials, an' bits falling orf. If we're lucky, there'll be a dockyard strike, or a fire in the officers' galley, or orl the wardroom down wi' food-poisoning the day before we're supposed ter sail.' The possibilities were endless.

'An' the Master-at-Arms stepping on a gangplank that ain't bleedin' there,' Steevo savoured, 'an' clewing up on the bottom of the dock like strawberry jam.'

Gibraltar first, Lobby Ludd hoped. It would be a cruel twist of fate to find himself back in Devonport, or even Walham Green, without a further opportunity for pursuing his understanding with Nurse McCudden, especially after having mastered the subjunctive and the indicative, and even more especially after being made Acting Yeoman of the Watch.

'Ludd and Smith,' the Chief had conceded reluctantly, as if the decision had been torn from him with hot irons, 'a desperate situation calls for desperate measures. I remember reading a book once about Napoleon's retreat from Moscow, and how all the gun-horses died, one by one – and how the men tied themselves to their guns an' hauled them through the snow, yard by yard, mile by mile, until they reached France. Thousands of 'em perished, see – but they saved the guns, so Napoleon could ride again.'

Smithie nodded soberly. 'But what's that got ter do with bleedin' dry dock, Chief? We ain't got no 'orses.'

'I mean, Smith,' the Chief Yeoman explained, 'that as there's only you, Ludd, Prettyman and me fit for flag-deck duty, we'll be reduced to three watches, single-handed; I'll stand by continuously.' He drew a deep breath. 'It don't matter how I change the names around, it comes out the same – bloody awful. You'll both be Acting Yeomen.' He winced. 'No, don't tell me you're touched by my confidence, Ludd. Just try to keep out of bloody trouble.'

'Don't you worry, Chief,' Lobby Ludd assured his senior. 'Adversity brings out the best in a man. If Smithie and me have to fight our way through shot and shell, dragging the ship behind us and dripping with blood, we'll get through.'

'That's what I mean,' the Chief grunted.

At three to four knots, *Bruno* had achieved only twenty miles when dawn filtered from the east, painting the horizon clouds first with flame, then purple, then mother of pearl. Cuniberti stopped engines to allow the roped lifeboats to be warped alongside while hot coffee was passed among them in a variety of receptacles. A haze of blue smoke rose from the open galley-hatch, and there was food, ill-assorted but welcomed – bread, tinned beef, cheese, reconstituted potato mash, a sack of apples. Men balanced on thwarts to urinate, to ease cramped legs. The night hours had not been punishing, but the men were stiff, chilled and hungry. Several gulls had appeared, floating above them in wide circles.

Spirits rose as the sun warmed and empty bellies were satisfied, and there was even a scattered exchange of chaff, but several men had died during the previous few hours. They included one of the badly burned men from *Susquehanna*'s boiler-room and a Polish corporal. There was nothing, however, to distinguish the corpses, wrapped and tied into blankets, as they lay on the fore-casing before being consigned to the sea. There were no salutes, no burial service. Cuniberti and Pedersen watched in silence as the weighted shapes sank from sight.

'Commander,' Pedersen said at last, 'a lot of things have happened in the last twenty-four hours, and I don't think anything can surprise me now, but where the hell do you think you're going? There's nowhere for you to run except a British or neutral port; you might as well have stayed put, and given these survivors a better chance. As of now, someone's going to die every hour and, anyway, your provisions can't last. Why don't you quit?'

Cuniberti, with his elbows on the bridge-screen, turned a tired face. 'Of course you are right, Captain. There is nowhere to run.' He sighed. 'You know, Captain, when I was a small boy in Montepascali, the old cat that caught the mice in my father's bakery she have five kittens. And my father say they must be drowned tomorrow. So, in the morning, I put the kittens into a box and ran away with the old cat following and crying. And I cried, too. But there was nowhere to run. It was raining, and soon I was hungry. After several hours I return home. My father say nothing, but he took the kittens and drowned them. After, he laughed and say that two of the kittens were dead already. And for days the old cat search everywhere, calling.'

Pedersen frowned. 'Commander—'

The Italian's voice was suddenly harder. 'A British cruiser was expected to reach your ship's boats during the early hours of this morning, Captain, but she has probably already been torpedoed. An American surface force is also closing, and will arrive during tonight or early tomorrow. Those survivors that are left after a battle has been fought over them with torpedoes and depth-charges, and have not died of wounds, thirst and exposure, will be picked up by a French squadron that left Dakar twelve hours ago.' He paused. 'The few we have here' – he waved an arm – 'are like my kittens in a box, Captain. I could not agree to attack the rescuing ships, but I could not just wash my hands. You will probably think of other things I might have done, but I could not betray my German allies, however much I disagree with them.' He shrugged finally. 'That is why, as you say, Captain, we have nowhere to run.'

The cloud was dispersing and the sun grew hotter. Cuniberti turned *Bruno* south-eastwards, towards the Cape Verde Islands, and by mid-forenoon there were shouts from the boats, telling of more deaths. Cuniberti stared at his chart, but it offered no solution. The supply of fresh water from the desalination plant was not meeting the constant demand, medical stores were exhausted, and food stocks were running alarmingly low. The radio operator had attempted to contact the French ships that had left Dakar, but failed. He did not know the French naval frequencies and there was no response on merchant-ship wavelengths. Burned and injured survivors under morphia sedation were beginning to regain agonizing consciousness, and there was nothing that could be done for them. Cuniberti had almost decided to turn about, to retrace his route, in the hope that Behrmann and Loerzer had failed to intercept the enemy's approaching rescue ships, but at precisely noon the future suddenly no longer mattered. Four aircraft screamed out of the thinning westerly clouds.

Both Cuniberti and Pedersen shaded their eyes. 'Avengers! *Americani!*' someone shouted. The aircraft were pale grey, in a tight echelon, and Pedersen nodded. 'That's right. They're Avengers. Well ...' The worst was over, and when the chips were down it had been American Navy fliers that had touched down, not British or French. Pedersen felt unusually patriotic, then recalled what Cuniberti had said about the German U-boats. At least the Avengers had taken off; he hoped there would be a carrier for them to re-land on. But there was nothing he could do except watch.

The lead plane banked, peeled away, followed by the second, the third, and then the tail-ender. Several Italian seamen were climbing from the open hatches, and all faces were turned upwards. There was no question of immediate rescue, Pedersen knew, but perhaps a parachute drop of survival packs, of drugs and dressings, a water-container, meat essence, concentrated soup, glucose, Lucky Strike cigarettes and Babe Ruth candy bars. The boats' position would be plotted, reported to the carrier, and then there would be more aircraft. If there was still a carrier.

The Avengers' approach was straight and fast – oddly fast for a parachute drop, Pedersen was thinking, and above the stubby, snub-nosed fuselage of the leader he could clearly see the heads of pilot and gunner. The bomb-bay was open. What was the sonofabitch doing? Anyone would think – and then his belly knotted.

A cluster of bombs detached themselves from the plane's underside and plummeted, as the Avenger, with an ear-splitting roar, hurtled overhead and away. 'Christ!' Pedersen shouted. The bombs seemed to float down excruciatingly slowly, and in the last moment before impact he flung himself to his knees with his arms over his head. The shudder of explosions and the engine-roar of the second aircraft were simultaneous. Cuniberti was still on his feet, hatless. 'Can't they see our Red Cross flag?'

The first stick of bombs had fallen short, slightly astern. On deck, seamen scrambled desperately for cover, and the trailing lifeboats lurched and tossed like corks as the sea convulsed. 'Let go the tow!' Cuniberti bellowed, but the second salvo had struck home. Pedersen felt the deck hammer against the soles of his feet. His ears sang. Godalmighty Jesus Christ, were the bastards blind? The air was thick with hot, acrid smoke, and Cuniberti still shouted for the tow to be slipped. Pedersen shot a glance astern just as the third stick of five 100-pound bombs struck the sea, full among the boats, saw the vomit of spray and splintered timber, the contorting shapes of men flung in every direction. The submarine yawed, rudderless, as the fourth Avenger screamed in.

He shook his fist at the air, incensed with frustrated rage. 'You moronic, murdering bastards!' he bawled, as the full pattern of bombs burst amidships.

nine

First Officer Jacobs sat with a blanket around his shoulders and his hands clenched around a cup of hot soup. 'The Wop submarine carried the name *Bruno*. She took off southwards, towing eight boats – and she had Captain Pedersen aboard. The two Kraut submarines carried no numbers, so far as I could see, and they embarked only senior Wehrmacht officers. I'd say they headed northwards initially, on the surface, but by that time it was dark. They could have altered course later.'

'One of them didn't,' Captain Mercer said, 'because he got a nasty shock, a couple of hours ago. It's my guess that his ugly brother is somewhere out there, gunning for us or TU17.4.' The signal from Admiralty, suffixed Immediate, had been received by *Daemon* only minutes before. *'Enemy U-boat group in your vicinity ordered to ignore rescue terms, to embark senior Wehrmacht survivors and then intercept and destroy British and American warships now closing.'* U-boat Command's original signal must have been transmitted in the Germans' complex U-boat code; there were probably dozens of such intercepted signals, addressed to the convoy battles in the North Atlantic, that competed for the attention of the Navy's code-breaking experts, and fifteen hours had elapsed. The American task group, however, would now have been warned.

'So we know what the Germans are up to,' Commander Plummer mused. 'But what about the spaghetti merchant? What the hell's he playing at?'

'When he slipped,' Jacobs recalled, 'he was showing a Red Cross flag. And with those boats in tow he can't be looking for a fight.'

Mercer grimaced. 'If he's not, and if he thinks he's doing a life-saving act, then God help him, because we can't. And if he thinks he's going to make a neutral port, or rendezvous with the French, he's not going to. The task unit's ETA is 10.00 tomorrow, and we'll have our hands full until then, but I'll suggest to the Americans that they make an air search as soon as they're within range, and then detach a destroyer. Chief

Yeoman, take a signal, please. To Task Group Seventeen Four from *Daemon* . . .'

It was 4 a.m. and only half-light. Seventeen crowded lifeboats, two motor-cutters and twelve Carley floats jostled for position at the lowered side-ladders and scrambling-nets, and hundreds of the chilled survivors were already aboard, the injured taken below to mattresses in the wardroom, officers' cabins and the bathroom flat, others herded forward to the mess-decks. There was a queue at the galley-hatch for kettles of hot cocoa and soup, and the smell of ether was already seeping from the chapel. A few German officers still retained sufficient arrogance to ask to be directed to the officers' quarters, and show indignation at learning that there was no segregated accommodation. As each boat emptied, its cocks were opened, and corpses were carried to the quarterdeck. From the bridge, Mercer and Plummer watched anxiously as boat after boat emptied, eyed the sky, the horizon. A stationary ship was helplessly vulnerable.

Major Quinn, filthy, unshaven, in his socks but grinning, came to the bridge. 'I was hoping you guys would get here first,' he confessed, 'and not a goddamn American with no liquor licence.' Colonel Dunlop, he told them, was below having broken ribs strapped and taking nourishment. Boleslavski had been missing since the torpedoing, but presumably Captain Pedersen was still alive. 'Some of the Poles and the crewmen are in good shape. Is there anything we can do, Captain?'

Mercer shook his head. 'Thank you, Major, but there's not much I can suggest. It's like Donnybrook Fair for the moment, and our most urgent concern is for getting under way as soon as possible. Somewhere out there' – he nodded at the sea – 'is an enemy U-boat with specific orders to destroy us. For all we know he may be sitting at periscope depth at this moment, watching us, and there's nothing we can do about it. So nothing much is going to matter until we empty these boats.'

'You mean all of them, Captain?' Jacobs asked. 'Hell, there must be more than three thousand—'

Mercer chuckled. 'This is a light cruiser, Mr Jacobs – not much bigger than an M-class destroyer, and we can't possibly accommodate three thousand passengers in addition to a crew of 450. But we will, because we can't stay here and we won't abandon any survivors. It's going to be very tight, and my First Lieutenant is going to play hell about the paintwork, but if we're lucky it will only be for twenty-four hours. I'm gambling on being able to transfer most of the survivors to the American carrier and cruiser. The nigger in the woodpile is this rogue U-boat that we know is around somewhere. We don't know the task group's precise whereabouts, or course, only that it should reach this position at 10.00 tomorrow – but I don't want the Americans to wireless any information that the enemy can intercept. So, when we've finished here, I'm going to steam westward, in the general direction of the task group's approach. We may make a radar contact. If not, we will rendezvous in this position tomorrow. I've already passed one signal, via ship–shore, informing the American commander of the Italian submarine's action and suggesting an air search. With luck, his aircraft might also surprise the German chappie on the surface – in which case we'll all be laughing, except Herr Kapitan.' He paused. 'And the Vichy French squadron? you are about to ask. Well, we aren't supposed to know, are we? They didn't tell us anything. It will be a nice little trip for them, after being tied alongside the jetty in Dakar for three years. They might even get their knees brown.'

It was sacrilege, Steevo stormed, to make tea in the rum fanny; his tot would never taste the same again. The rum fanny was exclusively for drawing rum. It was a bleedin' tradition going back to Nelson, and it was criminally unjust that every other artefact on the mess-deck had been requisitioned, including Steevo's hammock. It was that soddin' Master-at-Arms, whose alien parentage Steevo had always suspected. After the war, Steevo threatened darkly, there was going to be changes. And he'd bet the wardroom weren't all drinking their pink gins out of one bleedin' sugar basin. 'Jes' let me find a bloke in my 'ammock with his soddin' boots on, that's all,' he savoured, 'and I'll trim his bleedin' lamps.'

Lobby Ludd had no such reservations about the rum fanny. He had joined the long queue at the galley for hot water which, because of the heavy demand, was less than boiling, and the resultant anaemic brew, he speculated, would do little to improve Steevo's humour. He reached the flag-deck with his tepid prize just as the action alarm hammered. The Chief Yeoman was shouting and the 4-inch AA guns were lifting their muzzles. He had known the occasion before, and the feeling in the pit of his belly, the ashes in his mouth. It never failed. 'What's the buzz?' he asked Smithie, as if only indifferently interested.

'Aircraft approaching from north-west. They ain't likely ter be enemy – probably from the Yankee carrier. O' course, it won't make much difference if they don't know what a D-class cruiser looks like.'

'Ludd!' the Chief Yeoman roared. 'What's that? *Tea?* Do yer think this is bloody Ascot? Gawdstrewth. Where's yer parasol?' He drew breath. 'I have no desire ter appear unreasonable, Ludd, but we could be *fifteen seconds away from a bloody Stuka attack*!'

The four aircraft that had materialized from the northwestward were Avengers with American markings, in echelon. They swept in a wide circle as *Daemon*'s 4-inch guns tracked, turned away southwards, and within minutes had disappeared.

'W/T reports no joy on air–sea VHF, sir,' Lieutenant Cotton said. Commander Plummer grunted. 'I can never understand,' he frowned, 'why we can raise Portishead, Gibraltar, Malta and the Falklands as easy as spit, but we can never seem to communicate with an aircraft that's flying overhead.'

'Now the soddin' tea's got cold,' Smithie sniffed. Steevo choked into the sugar basin. 'Only it ain't tea, it's piss. In the bleedin' rum fanny.'

On her single screw, *Daemon* worked up to a cautious fifteen knots. If the American task group was still twenty-four hours away, Commander Plummer suggested, there would be little lost by a brief sweep to southward in the hope of overhauling the Italian *Bruno*, which, if still towing eight boats, could hardly have travelled fifty miles. Eight boats could mean three or four hundred survivors. *Daemon* already carried three thousand; she may as well go for a grand slam. The Italian's resources would be limited, and the poor devils in the boats could be suffering cruelly. Aircraft from USS *Peacock* might locate the submarine, but could do little except drop survival packs, if they carried them. A lot of the men in the open boats might not live through another day and night of exposure, and they included Americans and Poles.

Mercer considered. *Daemon* no longer resembled a warship. Her upper deck, every mess-deck, flat, cabin and passageway was crammed with survivors from *Susquehanna*. His own ship's company had abandoned their quarters and remained in the vicinity of their action stations; there was nowhere else to go. Major Quinn had mustered a platoon of Poles, and they had been issued with ship's rifles, but any realistic control of the teeming thousands of prisoners was inconceivable. It was possible only to keep them away from guns and torpedo-tubes, engine-room, and similarly sensitive areas. The prisoners were not obstructive, but neither were they particularly co-operative; they were sullenly resigned, like closely herded cattle. The Surgeon-Lieutenant and two German doctors had worked without pause in the makeshift casualty stations since dawn, and a week's supply of food, from galleys and bakery, had disappeared in the space of a few hours.

'This is worse'n the last steamer from Southend pier on a August Bank 'Oliday,' Smithie said. 'All we need is a few crates o' beer and a knees-up.'

'All right, Joe,' Mercer nodded. He looked for Lieutenant Cotton. 'Go south, young man. The Italian can only be hoping to narrow the distance between himself and the French, so he'll be heading for Dakar. Chief Yeoman, take a signal, please. "To Admiralty from *Daemon*, repeated C-in-C Med, US Chief of Naval Staff Med, Commander Task Group Seventeen Four: Have taken aboard three thousand plus survivors from *Susquehanna* in position already indicated but have suffered damage to one screw in successful action with enemy submarine. Speed reduced to fifteen knots and fighting ability impaired by overcrowding. Intend continuing southwards for eight hours in search of Italian submarine *Bruno* reported towing eight lifeboats and will rendezvous with TG17.4 to transfer survivors." '

The hot afternoon was barely an hour old when binoculars from *Daemon*'s bridge fastened on floating wreckage ahead.

'Smashed lifeboats, sir,' Lieutenant Cotton suggested. 'Planking, thwarts – and there's a stern-post and rudder.' First Officer Jacobs had come from below. Yes, he confirmed, *Susquehanna*'s boats had been grey-painted, but so were those of half the ships in the world. He couldn't be sure.

'Number One,' Mercer ordered, 'take a motor-boat away, please, and have a closer look for identification – a ship's name, life-jackets, papers – anything. Meanwhile, we'll circle. There may be more. Pilot, I'd like a position, please. And alert the Sick Bay.'

The SRE shrieked. *'First motor-boat's crew close up. Away first motor-boat.'* Mercer raised his binoculars again, but the Chief Yeoman was at his elbow. 'Operational Priority from Admiralty, sir.'

'To Daemon *from Admty: USS* Peacock *reports submarine attacked and destroyed by aircraft position 20.85 north 26.80 west at 1040z/08. In view your pick-up of* Susquehanna*'s survivors, TG17.4 will not repeat not rendezvous with you but will continue passage to Casablanca. Facilities at Bathurst inadequate for reception of 3000 survivors.* Daemon *should return Gibraltar if practicable, otherwise Freetown.* Bullfinch *is in your vicinity but if situation becomes critical* Swiftsure *will be sent to assist.'*

Mercer and Plummer gazed at each other. 'I don't believe it,' Plummer gritted. '"If situation becomes critical?" What the hell do they think it is *now*? We're reduced to one screw, we've got no radar, and we're loaded to the gunwales with POWs. Gibraltar must be all of sixteen hundred miles away and Freetown scarcely less. Whose bright idea do you suppose it is? Some Wren in the Admiralty's typing-pool?'

'That position given by *Peacock*, sir,' Lieutenant Cotton said quietly. 'Allowing for an element of drift, I'd say it's right here.'

Mercer nodded. 'Thank you, Pilot.' He walked to the bridge screen, fumbling for his pipe and narrowing his eyes against the sun-glare from the sea. The motor-boat was coming alongside.

Within minutes the First Lieutenant had climbed to the bridge. 'It's lifeboat wreckage, sir,' he reported, 'and possibly American mercantile pattern. Several boats, thirty-five-footers, carvel-built, but no markings.' He took a sodden, bulky white bundle from beneath his arm and allowed it to unravel, dripping, to the deck. 'And this, sir.'

It was a Red Cross flag.

It was as if Willis-Paget had tossed down the severed head of a negro; there was interest, but from a distance. Later, when the flag was hung to dry over the flag-locker, a number of ratings came to look at it. The Chaplain brought his camera, and asked Smithie to take his photograph, standing by the flag, after carefully explaining which hole to look through. 'If it comes out,' he confided, 'I may send it to the *Church Times*.'

'If it *comes out*?' Smithie snorted, when the Chaplain had gone. 'Shave off. Does he think I've never taken a bleedin' photo before? I've taken '*undreds* o' photos.'

'We ought to take a photo of *our* bloody Red Cross flag,' the Chief Yeoman muttered, 'and I'd send it to *Comic Cuts*.'

On the bridge, Mercer had decided not to turn for Gibraltar, 1,700 miles to the north-east. Facilities in the little port of Bathurst, on the Gambia, would be inadequate, but Freetown was 400 miles nearer than Gibraltar, and those miles could be vital. He had been tempted to make for Casablanca. He would like to see the Americans' faces when he came alongside with 3,000 Wehrmacht, and where did they want them put? But to hell with the Americans, and to hell with *Swiftsure*. He'd not give that *prima donna* another opportunity for some easy limelight.

'Pilot, make up a signal for Freetown, repeated Admiralty and C-in-C, will you? ETA, request berth alongside, and ambulances on arrival. I would like to off-load approximately three thousand prisoners to shore with minimum delay. That ought to have the Admiral's secretary twittering into his gin and mango juice. I don't care a damn if they're put into the Sierra Leone Hotel and the Wrennery, so long as they're off my ship. Fuel and store requirements to follow. Ah, yes – and request a diving party to stand by.'

Mercer frowned thoughtfully at the empty expanse of sea ahead. 'I've got that nagging feeling, Joe, that this thing's not finished. There's a loose end. What happened to that other U-boat? The devil's around here somewhere, we know what he's after, and he's probably got a better surface speed than we have. If we're not very careful, we could find ourselves right back where we came in. I hope you've paid your mess-bill.'

It was hot. Sun-glare off the sea stung the eyes, and exposed metal burned unwary flesh. Hundreds of prisoners sat or sprawled in areas of shade, slept, strolled, or sweated below on the crowded main deck where, with all scuttles open, the air was still thick with the smell of unwashed humanity. On the flag-deck, Lobby Ludd morosely scanned the horizon with binoculars, the Chief Yeoman sat with his back to the flag-locker. writing a letter, because the Chiefs' mess was occupied by Panzergruppe officers, and Smithie dozed with his cap over his face.

'What's there in Freetown', Lobby Ludd enquired, 'that we can't get in Gib, except coconuts?'

Smithie yawned and scratched an armpit. 'Naked black parties with rings in their noses,' he said. 'It'll make a change.'

'It's upset all my plans, that's all,' Lobby Ludd complained. 'I have to call on my fiancée, at the General Military Hospital.' He sniffed. 'She's an officer. But I'm not going to Spain this time. The last time, I nearly became a *cause célèbre.*'

'That could 'ave been nasty,' Smithie agreed. 'Still, they do bleedin' marvels with penicillin.'

'Do you think I ought to take flowers?' Lobby Ludd asked.

'Roses,' Smithie nodded. 'Them long-stemmed sods, like Michael Wilding always gives ter Anna Neagle. There's something about roses that makes wimmin lower their defences.'

Lobby Ludd considered. 'I really ought to wear civvies. I mean, it's a bit awkward – a matelot walking out with an officer. Not that she'd mind. She's not that sort. But we have to dine. I thought the Bristol.' He frowned. 'I could get a sports coat and flannels from Bernards.'

'And a bow-tie,' Smithie affirmed, 'and suede shoes. Y'know, if yer was a bit taller, and 'ad curly 'air, yer'd look a bit like Michael Wilding, not much, but a bit.'

The Chief Yeoman snorted. 'Do you blokes *have* to cackle? I've just written "Dear Michael Wilding".'

'As a matter of fact, Chief,' Smithie said seriously, 'I was only sayin' ter Lobby that, since yer ain't shaved, yer the spittin' image o' Ronald Coleman in *The Prisoner o' Zenda* – when he was in that dungeon fer a week—'

Before the Chief could explode, Lobby Ludd shouted. 'Chief, there's a flashing light – distant, port bow—' He frowned into his binoculars. 'There it is again – right on the horizon—'

Both Smithie and the Chief Yeoman were on their feet, shading their eyes. 'Are you sure?' The Chief stared. To the naked eye the horizon was empty, white-hot and shimmering.

'It's morse,' Lobby Ludd confirmed. 'S-O-U-S-M-A-R-I-N-A-V-A-N-T.' He paused, waited. 'That's all. It don't make sense, does it?'

The Chief looked at his writing-pad, on which he had pencilled 'Dear Michael Wilding sousmarinavant', peered again at the distant, empty horizon, and finally glared at Lobby Ludd. 'I don't know. But you'd better not be pulling my pisser, that's all, Ludd.'

'Sousmarin avant?' Commander Plummer glanced up quickly at the Chief Yeoman, then whirled, lifting his own glasses. 'Did you take a bearing, Ludd? And you're absolutely sure? It was just that, and nothing else?'

'Red oh-two-oh, sir – and that was all. It was only just visual, and it didn't seem like it was directed at us—'

'You're damned right it wasn't, Ludd,' Plummer grunted. 'Number One, port twenty and full ahead, please. Pipe hands to quarters without sounding the action alarm, will you? We don't want to stampede the prisoners. Warn Asdic to be on their toes. Ah, Captain, sir.' He grinned as Mercer appeared. 'Someone out there' – he nodded – 'has just flashed "Submarine ahead" to somebody else, in French. I thought you might like to investigate.'

Mercer patted his pocket for his pipe. 'That's interesting.' He nodded at the Chief Yeoman. 'Well done, Chief. Who saw it? Ludd? Well, I'll be damned. Whenever there's an international imbroglio, it always seems to revolve around Signalman Ludd.'

'There's smoke ahead, sir,' Lieutenant Cotton reported, 'and a foretop, I think, hull down.' Minutes later the ships were just visible – a cruiser followed by three smaller vessels in line ahead, ploughing northwards. 'Hell, they must be burning old tyres.' Beyond the distant formation was a spreading haze of brown smoke. 'It's them all right, sir – la Marine Nationale Française, out of Dakar. Do you suppose they know this is deep water?' He paused. 'The cruiser's flying a *contre-amiral*'s flag at her main, sir, which means she's our senior. Are you going to salute?'

'We're not on speaking terms,' Mercer said. 'The thing is they've just sighted a submarine, but they're not going to tell us. Asdic, what's the situation?'

'Asdic to bridge. Sweeping, sir. No contact.'

Mercer raised his binoculars. 'The Frenchmen couldn't have been making all that smoke, could they? I think we'll take a look at what's behind it. Pilot, bring us around, please.'

ten

For several hours *Oberleutnant* Ernst Loerzer had been perplexed and becoming angry. There had been no intelligence from BdU for the Markgraf group, only an endless stream of signals for the North Atlantic. Nor had there been any communication with U-157 at any of the pre-arranged transmission times. Loerzer would have expected Behrmann to have reported to Befehlsaber der Unterseeboote the sinking of the British cruiser by now, but perhaps Behrmann was keeping silent for tactical reasons; the British had become diabolically clever in their code-breaking and direction-finding activities. Still, a cruiser sunk would have made welcome news at German breakfast-tables, to help balance the grim bulletins from Russia. The Italian, *Bruno*, had vanished, but the Italians had always been fair-weather partners, and Cuniberti had only been true to his type. At dawn both ocean and sky were empty on all sides.

If only, Loerzer fretted, he knew more about the approach of the American task group. A carrier, a cruiser and three destroyers could pose problems for a lone submarine; he needed Behrmann, and he wished there had been time for closer consultation before they had both hurriedly abandoned *Susquehanna*'s lifeboats. Loerzer, like Behrmann, had Wehrmacht officers below deck – twenty-four of them, including four major-generals – who were becoming impatient with a situation they did not understand and conditions of confinement that were almost insufferable. They might not admit it, but most would have preferred that *Susquehanna* had been allowed to reach the United States unharmed, but since the transport had been sunk, and since they had exchanged captivity for the doubtful sanctuary of a submarine, they saw no reason why Providence should be tempted further. U-759 should run for home.

At ten in the forenoon, with still no sightings, Loerzer decided to circle back in the direction of *Susquehanna*'s lifeboats. He had barely altered course when a lookout screamed a warning of approaching aircraft. Loerzer glimpsed them as he flung himself at the upper hatch – four specks against the white tumble of cloud to the far north-west – and the ballast-tanks roared as the U-boat plunged. Loerzer took her deep, to ninety metres, and they waited tensely for the shudder of bombs. A crash-diving submarine left a telltale swirl on the surface that did not disperse for several minutes, but as each agonizing minute passed there was nothing. 'Seagulls,' someone laughed, but Loerzer knew he had seen aircraft. Submerged still, he continued eastwards until satisfied that the danger of attack had passed, ordered periscope depth, and then surfaced cautiously.

This, Loerzer calculated, was the approximate position of the *Susquehanna* torpedoing, but there was not a lifeboat in sight, and visibility was excellent. There was flotsam spreading for miles – all the broken debris from the sunken transport that had floated here twelve hours earlier – but of the dozens of heaving boats and life-rafts, choked with miserable humanity, there was not a sign.

It was baffling. Loerzer began a mile-by-mile search to windward, then circled yet again. At noon he fixed his position by sextant and chronometer with meticulous care and, precisely on the hour, risked a direct radio call for U-157. The earlier arrangement with Behrmann had been that, every fourth hour, the operators of both submarines would key their callsigns three times – a transmission too brief to be pounced upon by enemy D/F but sufficient for each U-boat to know that the other was operationally active. The last such contact with U-157 had been at midnight; there had been only silence at 04.00 and 08.00.

There was only silence now. 'Nothing, sir,' U-759's operator told Loerzer, standing at his shoulder. 'It could be an equipment failure, sir, but if you were to ask me ...'

Loerzer returned to the bridge to stare, puzzled, at an empty seascape. Had he been right in deciding that U-157 had sunk the British cruiser during the early hours? Or had the British been fiendishly clever? Something considerably larger than a submarine had plucked 3000 survivors from the sea – no mean feat under any circumstances – during the few hours that Loerzer had been idling just over the horizon. It was infuriating. How could it have happened? BdU would demand an explanation. The whole operation, so neatly parcelled, now seemed to have disintegrated, and Loerzer was feeling very lonely. Whoever had picked up the survivors, British or American, would now be racing for cover, and he would never catch them even if he knew where they were going. Perhaps the sulky Wehrmacht officers below were right. Perhaps U-759 should turn for home.

No, that was nonsense. Loerzer thrust aside his pessimism. There was still the American task group. The aircraft he had seen earlier *must* have come from a carrier, and U-759 still carried her full complement of twelve torpedoes. The whereabouts of *Susquehanna*'s survivors was irrelevant; whatever their fate, they could never have regained Germany.

All that he, Loerzer, had to do was wait. He was confident that he could penetrate an American destroyer screen and, having done so, he would loosen a salvo of four torpedoes at the carrier at point-blank range, then go deep immediately, under the escorts' noses. If the Americans lived up to their reputation, they would all be in the hangar watching a Hollywood film and chewing gum when the bottom fell out of their ship.

U-759 waited, cruising slowly, through the hot afternoon

and into the evening, and Loerzer watched the golden sky darken to rose, to purple velvet scattered with stars. Short-wave reception of Berlin Radio was excellent. There was dance music from the Adlon Hotel, Wagner, and military bands, punctuated by frequent, optimistic news bulletins. On the Eastern Front the Russian hordes had been halted, and a massive German counter-offensive was about to be launched. The British and American armies were being bled to death in Tunisia. A half-million tons of enemy shipping had been sunk in the Atlantic during March, and a whole new armoury of weapons was being amassed, including revolutionary fighter aircraft against which the Flying Fortresses would be helpless, and a colossal towing-glider, *Giganten.* Reception faded, distorting, as the dawn arose, but Loerzer had no further time for music or news bulletins. There was smoke on the horizon.

Not, however, to the north-west, where Loerzer had been expecting it, but on precisely the opposite bearing. It was incomprehensible. 'Dive,' Loerzer ordered. 'Periscope depth. Action stations.' There was ample time. He watched the needle of the depth-gauge until the roar of flooding tanks ceased and there was silence. He was going to make absolutely certain – not like Behrmann, who had blazed away like a drunk at a fun-fair.

'Propeller noises astern, sir. Several vessels. Closing.'

'Thank you,' Loerzer acknowledged. 'Up periscope. Flood tubes one to four.' But he was going to make absolutely certain.

As the periscope cleared he saw the ships immediately, despite the morning haze – two, three, four steaming in line ahead, but none had the distinctive shape of an aircraft carrier. The leader, the largest in the line, was a long-hulled warship with flared bows, raked, black-cowled funnels and a compact but impressive superstructure. 'French,' Loerzer breathed, and swore. It was the cruiser *Gloire*, he guessed, and following must be the two sloops and a gunboat that had accompanied her from Dakar and Konakry.

He straightened slowly. 'Dive. Forty metres.' There were questioning eyes on him as he watched the gauge-glass. 'It's the French squadron, and a beautiful target, but not for us. I don't think there's any need for them to know we're here. We'll let them get well clear.' Until now, he had hardly given a thought to the French, and they had got here a lot faster than he had expected. For the moment he could not quite decide what their arrival meant, except that it was an added complication. What the hell had happened to Behrmann?

'Propeller noises on port beam, sir. Constant.'

He nodded. The Vichy ships were on a wild goose chase, but that was not his concern. He would give them fifteen minutes.

'Propeller noises moving ahead, sir. Fading.'

Squeezed against the bulkhead of the control-room several sweating Wehrmacht officers watched events with strained faces. Well, Loerzer mused, they'd have a story to tell when they got home, and they would never again complain that the Kriegsmarine had a soft life while the Army bled and died in Russia and Africa.

The hydrophone operator's voice was suddenly urgent. 'Propeller noises astern, sir. Faint but closing.'

Loerzer jerked. 'Astern? Are you sure? Bearing?'

'Two-oh-oh, sir ... Two-oh-five. Distant. There's no doubt, sir.'

Loerzer directed a chuckle in the direction of the Wehrmacht officers. 'Well, well. It seems we have an unexpected guest.' He turned. 'Blow tanks. Periscope depth.'

It required seven or eight minutes before the contact materialized visually, far on the port quarter. Loerzer beckoned his First Lieutenant. 'Berthold, what do you make of that?'

Berthold had his eyes to the periscope mask for a long time. 'It looks like a sea-going tug, sir – or some sort of auxiliary. Single funnel, grey-and-blue camouflage. No armament to speak of. There's a 20mm mounting on the stern, and I think a couple of machine-guns just forward of the bridge. That's all.' He paused, then grinned. 'And she's flying a British ensign.'

Loerzer nodded. 'Shadowing. The Brits must be scraping the bottom of the barrel, but I imagine the North Atlantic has drained off all their better-quality ships.' He gazed at his subordinate thoughtfully, aware that every word was being anxiously devoured by his listening passengers. 'She's small fry, but she could be a hindrance, Berthold, so we'll have to sink her. But we're not wasting torpedoes on a sea-going tug. Stand by gun's crew. We'll engage with the 88mm, outside the range of her pea-shooter.'

Lieutenant George Chappell, RNVR, commanding HMS *Bullfinch*, had been a very surprised and somewhat apprehensive young man when he had been ordered out of Bathurst by a signal from the Admiralty via Freetown. He had never received an Operational Priority signal before in his entire naval career, and none at all from the Admiralty. It was all very dramatic, but he did not remotely expect just how dramatic things were going to become.

Bullfinch, of 498 tons, had been built as a deep-sea tug, but since the beginning of the war had been designated a coastal minelayer. She had never laid any mines and, indeed, carried only twelve in her after well-deck. Nobody wanted mines laid in the vicinity of Bathurst, Gambia, and for the last two years *Bullfinch* had been engaged in vaguely defined harbour-defence duties and inshore patrolling, armed with no weapons other than a single Oerlikon and two elderly Lewis guns.

Twice a year an electrical officer came up from Freetown to test the mines' detonating circuits, play a few games of tennis and share a few gins. 'Those mines of yours,' he told Chappell, 'should be in a maritime museum. If you ever have to lay them, they'll probably blow your stern off. If you're wise, you'll go sick that day, and send your First Lieutenant.'

Also from Freetown came an occasional frigate, or a 'Kil'-class sloop of the Freetown Escort Force, the crews of which regarded *Bullfinch* with a degree of condescension perhaps not untinged with envy. Almost any one of them would have been better suited to shadow the Vichy French squadron departing Dakar and Konakry, but, when it happened, none of them had been within reach. Lieutenant Chappell hoisted his pennants, slipped his moorings, and steamed for the open sea.

Dakar was only a hundred miles northwards, and Chappell idled off-shore until *Gloire* and *Annamite* emerged from harbour, dipped his ensign respectfully, and fell astern. *Bougainville* and *Dumont d'Urville* came up within hours, just before dark. It was odd, Chappell realized, seeing a line of warships with full lights; they could probably be seen for fifteen miles – which was not a bad thing for *Bullfinch*, with a 'Cherub' log, a magnetic compass and dead reckoning.

Chappell's orders were to 'contact and shadow', and he was not entirely sure what that implied. Presumably he was required to look for irregularities in the neutral warships' behaviour but, if he recognized any, he had no means of preventing them. The cruiser *Gloire*, and probably both sloops, could out-speed him easily if they wished. He had been told about *Susquehanna*, and it was comforting to know that every passing hour narrowed the distance between *Bullfinch* and the D-class cruiser *Daemon* – a big brother to whom Chappell would be relieved to transfer his responsibilities.

The first night had been calm, but heavily clouded and very dark, and he closed to within two miles of the French ships' stern-lights, falling back at dawn. The French ignored him, and he exercised action stations, uncovering his Oerlikon and two Lewis guns and pointing them in several directions, just to show the ships ahead that *Bullfinch* was at war, but they gave no sign that they were impressed. The day grew hotter. A long, uneventful afternoon became evening, then night again, with the sky clear and starry. There had been no signal traffic of relevance on Bathurst's port wave, on which reception was becoming difficult.

At dawn, yet again, nothing had changed. Something would have to happen soon, Chappell speculated, or he would be steaming off his chart. Then something did happen. A submarine surfaced, three miles off *Bullfinch*'s starboard bow.

Chappell was not aware that there were any British submarines nearer than Gibraltar or Trincomalee, but it was equally unbelievable that this was a real enemy U-boat. In sun-drenched, lazy Bathurst such a possibility was remote. There were destroyers, frigates, and even 'Kil'-class sloops which were equipped, trained and eager to fight U-boats; it was totally unjust that, when one appeared, it should be confronted by a sea-going tug whose only resemblance to a warship was its shabby white ensign. But there was no time for deliberation, and Chappell did three things very quickly. He sounded the action alarm, rang for emergency full speed, and called for maximum port rudder. Ten seconds later all doubt disappeared as a shell struck the sea only fifty yards astern, erupting.

Chappell's immediate thought was that he ought to have left the two native messboys ashore in Bathurst, because it was highly unlikely that *Bullfinch* could escape from an enemy with a gun that considerably out-ranged her and a speed six or seven knots faster. He ought to make an enemy report by W/T. Perhaps he ought to open fire with the Oerlikon; it was better than doing nothing. *Bullfinch*'s single funnel poured smoke as she turned, obscuring his sighting of the surfaced submarine, and he was not quite sure of her bearing. Then another shell burst, again astern, and uncomfortably closer.

His second-in-command, Sub-Lieutenant Oram, had just scrambled breathlessly to the bridge with a large coffee-stain on the front of his shirt. 'Were they *real*?' he asked. 'Christ.' To the northward the four French ships had continued on course, apparently unperturbed. There was a third shell-burst, and Chappell could see the U-boat again. He could swear she was overhauling.

Then he remembered the smoke canisters. Simultaneously Oram said, 'If one of those shells lands among our mines, it'll be "Goodnight, Nurse".'

Against *Bullfinch*'s stern-rails were two smoke canisters, each the size and shape of a garden dustbin. They were intended for diesel- and petrol-driven craft which could not generate smoke by the usual method of opening the fuel injection valves and over-feeding oil to the furnaces, but a few canisters were often surreptitiously acquired by oil-burning ships because making smoke was anathema to engine-room personnel. The canisters, which, according to a legend stencilled on their casings, 'If thrown overboard will float', were activated by a sharp blow by any weighty instrument delivered to a brass percussion cap, followed by a hurried retreat.

'Sub!' Chappell shouted. 'Make smoke! And jettison the mines!' Making smoke was an ostrich-like remedy; it would not stop the shells but at least it would hide where they came from. Oram nodded, turned, then hesitated. 'I'll need a hammer from somewhere,' he frowned. Chappell's language was obscene.

Oberleutnant Loerzer watched the first shell fall short as the enemy vessel turned frantically away. 'That's spoiled their breakfast,' he grinned. He had opened fire prematurely. The U-boat had no sophisticated range-finding system and the gun-crew enjoyed little opportunity for practice; he should have got closer. Still, it hardly mattered. 'He can't run far,' he told Berthold. He shot a quick glance in the direction of the French ships, disappearing northwards. 'Keep firing. And bring us nearer, Berthold.'

The second shell was also short, the third might have been a direct hit if the enemy had not been still turning. Then Loerzer swore. 'The devil's making smoke.' He lifted his binoculars. 'Smoke canisters, on the stern. Well, it's not going to save him.' It was annoying – the penalty for surfacing at a distance. The Brit was only delaying the inevitable, but he would have time to transmit an enemy report. 'Full ahead both. We'll come up to windward.' Loerzer had all day, the conditions were perfect, and the nearest sanctuary was 200 miles away. Even so, he did not wish to prolong the action unnecessarily. There were enemy aircraft around, and he could become the biter bitten.

The smoke was chocolate brown, dense, and acrid in the nostrils, floating a few feet above sea-level. From the bridge of U-759, knifing through the sea at eighteen knots, Loerzer glimpsed the enemy ship momentarily as it twisted away again. 'Those smoke canisters float,' he shouted at Berthold. 'He might try dropping them astern, to keep us guessing.' He pointed ahead. 'There – I thought so ...' A small dark shape rose and fell in the low swell still churned by the enemy ship's screws, wreathed by smoke. 'And there's another—'

There was a shuddering roar, the deck lurched under him, and, incredulous, he saw the gun-crew below spilling in all directions. Under the U-boat's bows the sea had erupted, and the raft container on the casing had been flung aft, to shred itself on the 88mm. Berthold rose to his knees, his nose bleeding, dazed, and Loerzer stared ahead, still unbelieving. 'What the hell happened?' he choked. 'We've lost our bows.'

Hundreds of prisoners had crowded *Daemon*'s rails to watch the passing of the French squadron, which was now disappearing northwards, and now they scattered for cover as smoke began to sting their throats and eyes. Mercer held a handkerchief to his mouth. 'This isn't boiler smoke, Joe. What the hell is it? Pilot, don't take us into the stuff; get us to windward.' A moment later he stiffened. 'Was that gunfire?'

'A four-inch or four-seven,' Plummer calculated. 'And there's another—' He coughed. 'This is chemical smoke, sir, from canister generators. Someone's laying a screen, but he's not maintaining course. He's turning.'

'Keep the smoke to starboard, Pilot,' Mercer ordered. 'Director, all guns independent, stand by to engage starboard side. We'll do a complete circuit. Sooner or later someone's got to come out.'

'If he doesn't vanish up his own rear orifice,' Lieutenant Cotton suggested.

'Main W/T to bridge. Preliminary enemy report, sir. All British Warships from Bullfinch. *One submarine. No position, course or speed, sir, but the transmission's blasting our heads off. It sounds like she's alongside.'*

The PO Telegraphist's voice was almost accusing.

'*Bullfinch*?' Mercer peered at the long, tumbling pall of smoke to starboard as *Daemon* heeled, turning. 'Good God. I'd forgotten all about *Bullfinch*. Didn't you say she'd only an Oerlikon and two Lewis guns, Pilot?'

'That's what the book says, sir,' Cotton nodded.

'All guns loaded, ready to fire.'

The report from the Director was followed almost immediately by a distant rumble, like that of brief thunder. 'That wasn't a four-inch,' Plummer said. 'It was a torpedo or a mine. I'd say *Bullfinch* has copped it.'

'Damn and buggery,' Mercer gritted. He threw an upward glance at the wrecked radar lantern and then at the deck forward, thickly thronged with Germans in their drab and dirty battle-dress. He knew that Major Quinn had fifty Polish infantrymen armed with rifles, another hundred with batons, positioned strategically throughout the ship, and Quinn himself stood at the after 20mm gun with an M1 automatic slung from his neck like a Chicago gangster, but it was impossible to predict what might happen if *Daemon* engaged an enemy ship.

'Still no Asdic contact, sir,' Cotton confirmed.

'All right. Reduce to slow. Starboard twenty. Joe, pipe all hands to keep their eyes peeled for *Bullfinch*, or a U-boat.' *Daemon* turned her bows into the smoke.

Sub-Lieutenant Oram raced from the well-deck to the bridge. 'Did you hear that explosion? It was one of the mines. The U-boat hit it.' He whooped. 'We've sunk a bloody U-boat!'

'We might have,' Chappell agreed, 'and we might not. We're not going back to find out.' He lowered his head to the voice-pipe. 'Coxswain, steer one-one-five.'

'But how will we know for certain?' Oram asked. 'What will you tell NOIC?'

'I'll tell him we heard a loud bang and the U-boat stopped firing. If he wants to know any more, the "Kils" can sort it out. They're supposed to be the experts. We're getting to hell out of here.'

Oram, however, was no longer listening. His jaw had dropped as he stared at the smoke that thinned momentarily ahead. 'Christ!' he shouted frantically. 'Look out! There's a bloody great cruiser passing across our bows!'

'A cruiser?' Chappell whirled. 'I can't see—'

Then he did. Less than fifty yards ahead, a long, pale-blue hull glided wraith-like out of the swirling smoke from right to left – bows and fo'c'sle, guns, bridge, funnels – indistinctly massive and only seconds away as *Bullfinch*'s engines thrust her through the water at her maximum 10½ knots. A siren howled, and Chappell flung himself at the voice-pipe again. 'Hard to starboard, full astern both!' Thirty yards, twenty. The minelayers turbines responded slowly as her screws threshed, and the great wall of the cruiser's hull, ahead, seemed endless as it slid to port. There was going to be a collision, Chappell knew with certainty. What the hell was a bloody cruiser doing here?

Bullfinch's bows tore obliquely and with a sickening crash into *Daemon*'s hull just below the cruiser's after torpedo-tubes, gouging a ragged, V-shaped gash in her plates before being wrenched free by the momentum of both vessels. There was a second, shuddering impact as *Bullfinch* swung her flank, and then she jolted along *Daemon*'s side, beam to beam, with protesting steel screeching. Chappell, clinging to the voice-pipe, was confusedly aware that the cruiser's shelter-deck was inexplicably crowded with shouting men, that triple torpedo-tubes with torpedoes loaded and suspended crazily had just smashed away his own lifeboat and davits and, finally, that there was sure to be a court martial and he had better start thinking about it.

'It was the wardroom,' Oram shouted.

'What?' Chappell gasped.

'We holed the wardroom. I could see the green carpet.'

eleven

'Ah, yes,' Smithie approved, when Lobby Ludd emerged from the changing-cubicle in Messrs Bernards. 'Very tiddley. Class.'

'You don't think the shirt's a bit flashy?' Lobby asked. 'I mean – lemon with brown stripes?'

'It ain't the shirt, mate,' Steevo sniffed. 'It's the roses. Yer'll look a ponce wi' a bow-tie and a bunch o' bleedin' roses.'

'Not with a dog-tooth check jacket,' Smithie shook his head. 'Yer can go anywhere in a dog-tooth check jacket. An' there's nothing poncey about a belt with a snake's 'ead buckle. I still think yer oughter 'ave an 'at, Lobby. If yer 'ad an 'at, yer'd look like an officer.'

'I wish I'd looked like an officer when we went to the Bristol.' Lobby said. There was not a table to be had for this evening, a polished under-manager had assured the three sailors, his eyes distant. Not a table. He was very sorry. Had they tried the Jubilee Seafood Restaurant in Line Wall Road?

'For the price of them soddin' roses,' Steevo calculated, 'yer could 'ave bought booze fer a week. D'yer know they were three bob *each*?' Roses, the exquisite young lady in Flower Fayre had said, were *very* difficult in Gibraltar, but he was lucky – she did happen to have a few Crimson Glories. Two dozen? Of course. And would he like a card? There was no extra charge for a card. 'I shouldn't soddin' think so,' Steevo snorted. 'Shave off. Yer'd better take out Third Party, Fire an' bleedin' Theft, mate.'

'Don' ferget, Lobby,' Smithie advised when they parted, 'if yer lines git fouled, we'll be in the El Morocco – me an' Steevo, an' Jan Prettyman an' Knocker.'

To Smithie's disgust, who had confidently predicted seven days' leave for each watch in the UK, and gleefully increased this to fourteen days after the collision with *Bullfinch*, *Daemon* lay in Gibraltar's no. 2 dry dock with scaffolding around her screws and the ragged hole in her port side that had been temporarily patched in Freetown. There were drums of pale-blue paint on the dockside – inferior wartime quality, the First Lieutenant lamented – and a working party was already chipping the old from the blistered funnels. On second thoughts, Smithie decided, it might have been better if *Bullfinch* had gone straight through the after boiler instead of the wardroom; there wouldn't have been such a bleedin' panic to get the ship into the nearest available dry dock. As it was, C-in-C Med had ordered, *Daemon* had precisely eight days in which to carry out repairs, provision, refuel, and be ready for sea. A quarter of a million enemy troops were about to surrender in Tunisia, and every transport and escort was going to be needed for the task of taking them out of North Africa.

'Not in *my* bleedin' 'ammock, mate,' Steevo had promised. *Daemon* had landed 3000 Wehrmacht survivors in Freetown, to be re-embarked in a troopship hastily summoned from Simonstown and, before departure, the Germans had systematically wrecked everything they surreptitiously could – electrical fittings, bathroom showers and mirrors, hoses, lockers, mess-traps – until the cruiser's below decks had the appearance of being ravaged by a typhoon. Steevo had lifted a potato he was peeling. 'When we win the bleedin' war' – he demonstrated

– 'we oughter castrate the soddin' lot of 'em.' The only consolation in the sorry sequence of events was that the wardroom had been flooded.

Captain Mercer's annoyance had been exacerbated by the fact that *Bullfinch* had survived the collision unscathed except for the loss of her whaler, while the massive cable fairlead in her bows had torn a hole in *Daemon*'s hull, wrenched the after torpedo-tubes from their mountings, and finally sheared away thirty feet of guard-rail and stanchions. Angrily, Mercer had hailed *Bullfinch*'s bridge, asking for information on the U-boat.

'I think we sank it, sir,' Chappell returned.

'You *think* you sank it?' Mercer demanded. 'With an Oerlikon?'

'We dropped our mines, sir,' Chappell tried to explain, 'and one of them must have lost its sinker—'

'You mean there are *mines* floating around here as well?'

'Well, only a few, sir – and they're not very reliable . . .'

There was a foot of brine in the wardroom, but the damage had been caulked with timber and a pump was already working. The smoke was dispersing, there was no sign of the U-boat, and Chappell wondered what he ought to do next.

'Do you think we might offer a tow?' Sub-Lieutenant Oram suggested. 'After all, this was a tug, once.'

It might not be diplomatic. 'We'd better wait until we're asked,' Chappell decided. *Daemon*, however, was not in need of a tow. 'Take station two cables astern,' her lamp ordered. 'Speed nine knots, course one-two-oh.'

'That's Freetown,' Oram protested. 'We don't want to go to Freetown, do we?'

'It's been my experience, Sub,' Chappell replied, 'that there're times when it's best to keep your mouth shut.'

Passage was resumed without further communication, but at noon another signal came from *Daemon*. 'Resume course for Bathurst. Report on earlier action should be made to C-in-C. Good luck.' *Bullfinch* acknowledged, turned thankfully away, anxious for the quiet sanctuary of the Gambia, uneventful inshore patrols and back in time for the 16.30 dockyard bus.

In Freetown there were shaken heads and tongue-clicking over *Daemon*'s damage. Yes, a temporary patch could be welded over the hole in the hull, but as for the screw, the radar and the torpedo-tubes – well, Gibraltar was better equipped. It was a question of spares, which might take weeks to arrive. All speculation, however, had been terminated by C-in-C Med. Return to Gibraltar forthwith. Mercer, with good grace, had accepted the company of a radar-equipped sloop – a precaution that had amused *Swiftsure*, alongside the wall, as the battered *Daemon* entered Gibraltar harbour. 'I see they've brought you back, then,' *Swiftsure* flashed. 'You really ought to look where you're going.'

Eight days, the Commander and the First Lieutenant agreed, was impossibly brief. The only answer, reluctantly, was to reduce shore-going to a minimum and have the hands working throughout every day until repairs were finished. Approached with the suggestion, Captain Mercer was equally reluctant. He frowned, but conceded that there was little alternative if C-in-C's deadline was to be achieved. 'Well, all right,' he nodded. 'No shore leave until the job's done, except for compassionate cases, by request. And that means officers, Joe. I don't want to see any officers swanning ashore, under any pretext, while the hands are confined to ship. In fact, nobody will leave the ship without my personal authorization.'

'Would you soddin' *believe* it?' Smithie howled, when the announcement was piped. 'No bleedin' shore leave? What's the good of getting yerself damaged if yer don't get shore leave? Shave off.'

'You jes' wait, mate,' Steevo threatened darkly. 'I'm goin' ter write ter my soddin' MP. It's a diabolical bleedin' liberty.'

Lobby Ludd gazed at the soaring mountain of rock beyond the dockyard buildings and terraced roofs in the direction of the General Military Hospital. 'This,' he lamented, 'could be the death knell of my marital aspirations.'

The Chief Yeoman, whose humour during the past week had been so bland that Smithie hoped he might be sickening for something, eyed his subordinates thoughtfully for several moments, then snorted, 'We'll bloody see about that,' and strode from the flag-deck.

'I knew it, mate,' Smithie breathed. 'He's gone round the bleedin' bend. It must 'ave been the sun.'

The Chief Yeoman went below, changed into his best suit and, with his cap under his arm, knocked on the door of the Captain's sea-cabin. As he entered, Paymaster-Lieutenant Gasnier was departing. There was a relieved expression on his face. Captain Mercer looked up from a table cluttered with papers. 'Is it important, Chief?' he asked. 'Can't it wait?'

'If you don't mind, no, sir,' the Chief said, and closed the door firmly behind him. 'It's about shore leave—'

Mercer held up his hand. 'Before you go any further, Chief, you might like to know that Lieutenant Gasnier has just come from the dockyard signals office with this.' He brandished a signal. 'It's from C-in-C. Our earlier orders have been cancelled.'

'Cancelled, sir? Does that mean—?'

'It means, Chief, that *Swiftsure* will assume responsibility for our programme – which her captain won't like a bit. She'll be slow-convoying to Malta for the next two months. C-in-C has decided that eight days aren't enough to get us ship-shape, and now we have three weeks. That makes a lot of difference. When I've had a word with the Commander, I'm sure he'll be piping leave – and that probably means you'll be ashore at thirteen-thirty.' He smiled. 'Does that solve your problem?'

The Chief Yeoman grinned in return. 'Well, it wasn't so much my problem, sir. It was my flag-deck ratings. I wouldn't tell them to their faces, but they've had a green rub – watch-keeping till they were near dead on their feet, then no reliefs and no leave.' He shrugged. 'O' course, they never stopped moaning, but that's what kept them going. I was going to ask that you treated them as compassionate cases, sir, and allow them a run ashore. They've earned it. One of them, anyway, has his fiancée here – and I suppose that's compassionate.'

'Here? In Gibraltar? Who's that?'

'Signalman Ludd, sir. I understand she's a nurse at the General Military Hospital.'

'A nurse at GMH? Really?' It was a coincidence. Only a few minutes before, Lieutenant Gasnier had also requested to be allowed a few hours ashore on the grounds that his fiancée was a nurse at the General Military Hospital. Mercer chuckled. 'Well, I suppose we can thank Ludd for sighting that French submarine report, which led to us getting holed. And what's the point in getting us damaged if he doesn't get some leave out of it?'

Five minutes later the Chief Yeoman reappeared on the flag-deck. 'You lot,' he scowled, 'are the idlest bloody shower I've ever met. *What* are you, Ludd?'

'The idlest bloody shower you've ever met, Chief,' Lobby Ludd agreed.

'And there's going to be some *smartening up*,' the Chief promised. 'Before we leave this dock I want the flag-deck painted, all the flags dhobied and new halyards rigged. That's just for starters. Every forenoon there'll be a flashing and hoisting exercise, questions on the Fleet Signal Book, and aircraft recognition. We might even do it in gas-masks.'

His scowl deepened. 'I have just had a blast from the Captain over you lot, and I took all the blame. I was *blasted*. I probably shan't get my Good Conduct Medal next year, all because of you lot.'

Smithie and Lobby Ludd were suitably shamefaced.

'In spite of all that,' the Chief gritted, 'I spoke up for you, see. I pleaded. The Captain told me not to be a bloody fool – not to throw my career away on a stroppy bunch of skates like you. "You'll never get gratitude", he said, "from the likes of them." '

'Sorry, Chief,' Lobby Ludd offered.

The Chief Yeoman sighed, looked at his watch, then regarded them with narrowed eyes. 'There's just time for you to shave and change. You've all got watch-keepers' leave from thirteen-thirty.'

It was a long, warm walk up Europa Road to the General Military Hospital. His new shoes pinched, and the Crimson Glories were beginning to look a little jaded. At the hospital gate there was a confusion of signs ordering Drive Slowly, Keep Off the Grass, No Dogs Allowed, and Do Not Park on Yellow Lines, with all of which Lobby Ludd complied. Thirty yards within, the driveway offered a choice of two routes, one to Officers' Reception and Sun Lounge (Officers Only) and the other to Other Ranks and Infectious Diseases. Eventually he located the Nursing Officers' Residence: Authorized Personnel Only.

In the immaculate marble and polished-oak hallway yet another notice announced No Visitors Beyond This Point, Ring Once and Wait, and No Smoking. Lobby Ludd rang once and waited, and then a voice from an easy chair, feet away, said, 'Good heavens. It's Ludd, isn't it? What are you doing here, Ludd? Have you got compassionate reasons?' It was Paymaster-Lieutenant Gasnier.

Lobby Ludd was equally surprised. He was about to respond when there was another interruption.

'Geoffrey, darling. How marvellous. How absolutely wonderful.' Nurse McCudden flung her arms around Lieutenant Gasnier's neck and kissed him very fervently. Lieutenant Gasnier kissed her back, and Lobby Ludd studied his shoes, which were pinching more than ever. He ought to have got a larger size.

'When I heard that *Daemon* was in harbour,' Nurse McCudden went on breathlessly, 'I knew you'd come if you could.' She kissed Lieutenant Gasnier again, and then suddenly became aware of Lobby Ludd. Her eyes widened.

'Why, it's Mr Ludd.' She stared. She glanced at Lieutenant Gasnier. 'Did you come together?'

'No,' Lieutenant Gasnier assured her. 'We didn't.'

There was a moment of silence. Nurse McCudden frowned. 'You didn't come to see me, did you?'

Lobby Ludd shrugged. 'I happened to be passing, and I just happened to have this bunch of roses that I didn't want. "A hospital!" I said to myself. "Now, that's a coincidence"—'

'Roses,' she smiled. 'We never have roses. They're so expensive. It's very nice of you, Mr Ludd – isn't it, Geoffrey?' Lieutenant Gasnier grunted, and Nurse McCudden squeezed his arm. 'I'll put them in the Zymotics Ward.'

There was another silence. Lieutenant Gasnier cleared his throat. 'Well, if that's all, Ludd ...?'

'Next time,' Nurse McCudden said, as Lobby Ludd turned to go, 'you can always leave anything in reception, to save waiting.'

'Sometimes these lower-deck ratings baffle me.' Lieutenant

Gasnier shook his head, then brightened. 'I thought we'd dine at the Bristol. I've got a table.'

'Wotcher, me ol' mate,' Smithie greeted, as Lobby Ludd entered the seedy El Morocco. 'We're all drinkin' black an' tans, and yer about five pints adrift. It's Steevo's round.'

''Ow can it be my soddin' round,' Steevo protested, 'when I bought the one before this? D'yer think I'm bleedin' dense?'

'Soddin' 'ell,' Lobby Ludd winced. 'My bleedin' feet. They're murder. I ain't never walkin' up that soddin' road again, mate, I can tell yer. I'd never 'ave gone if I'd bleedin' known. It's worse'n jankers.' He took a generous mouthful of beer, then sighed. 'Bleedin' marvellous.'

'Cheers,' Smithie said.

'Ah, yes,' chuckled the Master-at-Arms, at the door. 'Signalman Ludd, in civilian clothes. And a bow-tie, too. Very tiddley.' Behind him waited two patrolmen in belts and gaiters. 'Of course, Ludd, yer do know that ratings ain't allowed ter wear civilian clothes ashore in Gibraltar without express permission *in writin'* from the Commanding Officer? You do? And you ain't got permission?' He shook his head sadly. 'Well, well. I reckon we'll jes' take a little stroll back to the ship, Ludd, and then visit the quarterdeck.' He sniffed. 'And let's see if the Matron phones up about this.'

Glossary of Naval Lower-deck Terminology and Technical Terms

Many Naval expressions have passed into common use and their original meanings have become blurred. Many others, from sailing-ship days, have passed into misuse. Those listed below were common during the Second World War, and undoubtedly some still survive.

The list is, of course, by no means complete, but expressions and abbreviations used in the text are included, together with one or two others which give the flavour of the period.

Nicknames have not been included because they were so numerous. A Williams was inevitably a 'Bungy', Wilson a 'Tug', Bell a 'Dinger' and every Knight a 'Bogey'. Ships also had their nicknames. *Royal Sovereign* was the 'Tiddley Quid', *Vengeance* was the 'Lord's Own' ('Vengeance is Mine, saith the Lord. I will repay') and *Weston-super-Mare* became 'Aggie on Horse-back' – a subtlety that the reader can unravel for himself by referring to the notation against 'Aggie Weston'.

AB Able Seaman.
Active Service Term applied to ratings of the regular Navy although, contrarily, they were of peacetime recruitment.
adrift Late, particularly when mustering or returning from leave.
Aggie Weston Loosely applied to all seamen's temperance hostels ashore, but particularly those originally introduced by Dame Agnes Weston, the 'sailors' best friend', who, however, also persuaded the Admiralty to stop issuing rum to ratings of under twenty years.
all night in For watchkeeping sailors, the occasion on which they enjoyed an entire night in their hammocks. Ashore, all night abed with a woman.
Ally Sloper's Favourite Relish A particularly racy bottled sauce, available from ship's stores, reputed to be excellent for cleaning brasswork.
Andrew (The) The lower deck's name for the Royal Navy. During the Napoleonic Wars, Andrew Miller was a notorious press-gang officer who impressed so many seamen that he was said to own the Navy.
Asdic Submarine-detection branch, equipment and techniques. From the initial letters of the Anti-Submarine Detection Investigation Committee of 1917.
ATS Auxiliary Territorial Service, former name of the Women's Royal Army Corps.

baby's head See 'dead baby'.
back teeth awash Drunken, or the process of becoming so.
BAMS Wireless broadcast service for British and Allied merchant ships.
baron One with modest accumulation of money, usually by saving, and a target for borrowers.
battle-wagon Battleship.
bear pit The stokers' messdeck.
belay Stop or cancel. To 'belay the last pipe' would be a cancellation of the last order given.
bells Bell-bottomed trousers, sometimes worn extravagantly wide in defiance of regulations.
Blue Label Popular brand of bottled beer, brewed in Malta.
Bluenose One who has travelled north of the Arctic Circle. Circumstances permitting, first-timers are subjected to a light-hearted ceremony similar to that when crossing the Equator, and presented with a 'Bluenose certificate' signed by the ship's captain.
BN Continuous wireless broadcast for warships, 107 kc/s.
boatswain's pipe A whistle blown by boatswain or quartermaster to precede orders given to crew or watch, or as a salute to senior officer or another ship. Today, most orders or announcements are broadcast over the ship's amplifier system.
Bootnecks Royal Marines, for whom sailors had little affection.
breathing licence Station card – an identity card held by all ratings, deprival of which meant loss of leave and limitation of leisure activities.
bubbly Rum, issued to eligible ratings daily.
Buffer; Chief Buffer Bosun's Mate; Chief Bosun's Mate.
bulkheads The dividing walls of below-decks compartments.
bunting General term for flags of all kinds.
bunting tosser, Bunts Rating of Visual Signalling Branch.
buzz Rumour, often distorted by repetition or completely unfounded.
buzzer Closed-circuit morse code for practice purposes.
BWO Bridge Wireless Office.
cable (length) Unit of distance, about 200 yards.
Captain D Senior officer of destroyer flotilla.
Carley floats Life rafts of varying sizes, often made of balsa.
caterer Senior rating in mess, once responsible for victualling arrangements.
Charlie (Chaplin) Ship's chaplain. Padre.
Chinese wedding-cake Boiled rice, laced with currants.
Chippy Ship's carpenter.
chocker Fed up, frustrated. Abbreviation of 'chock-ablock', meaning a rope that is jammed tightly into its block.

civvies Civilian clothes.
Civvy Street Civilian life, the yearned-for end of a service engagement.
clacker Pastry or pie crust.
cleaning station Appointed location for daily cleaning duties.
clew up Finish, end up. A defaulter might 'clew up' in goal.
coaming Vertical erection around hatch or at base of door to prevent entrance of water.
Cook of the Mess Rating(s) responsible for bringing food from galley, washing up, cleaning messdeck.
corned dog Corned beef.
cowboys Bacon and beans.
crusher Regulating Petty Officer (RPO), member of Naval police branch, allegedly the last resort of the moronic or illiterate.
daymen Ratings who do no watchkeeping and work during day hours only, thus enjoying 'all night in' every night.
dead baby Sometimes 'baby's head'. Meat pudding.
deckhead The ceiling of any below-deck area.
depot Devonport, Portsmouth and Chatham were depots, also port divisions, to one of which every rating belonged, defined by the letter D, P or C prefixing his official number.
DFs Duty Frees, referring to duty-free cigarettes or tobacco.
D/F Direction finding.
dhobeying The process of washing clothes.
dickie White linen bib-like item, secured by tapes, worn instead of a standard seaman's shirt.
dip, at the 'At the dip!' was a response when addressed or called; an acknowledgement. An ensign was dipped in salute or acknowledgement of another.
ditty box Small box of scrubbed white wood, with brass name-plate and lock, in which a rating kept his most private possessions, letters, photographs, etc.
divisions Morning muster of ship's company.
DNO Director of Naval Operations.
DO Divisional Officer, of which there might be a number in a ship, each responsible for different professional branches.
draft chit Drafting instructions to or from a ship or foreign station.
drills White drill uniform.
drink, the The sea, particularly that in close proximity; e.g., '. . . fell into the drink'.
ducks See 'Number Threes' for definitions of naval kit.
EA Electrical Artificer.
EDR Electrical Distance Recorder.
ENSA Entertainment National Service Association; a wartime

organization providing travelling concert parties for the armed services.
ERA Engine Room Artificer.
ETA Estimated Time of Arrival.
fearnought Stout, felt worsted cloth, fire-resistant, once used for stokers' trousers but more latterly to reinforce damage-control plugs and for fire-fighting.
Fill your boots! Help yourself!
filled in Suffer bruises or beating in fight or brawl.
fish-heads Aircraft carrier's ship's company, as opposed to Fleet Air Arm personnel. (See 'pin-heads'.)
flakers Exhausted. To 'flake out' is to collapse.
flannel (1) Seamen's white flannel shirt, with square-cut neck edged with blue jean. (2) Nonsense, unconvincing bluster.
flat aback Cap worn on back of head, contrary to regulations.
flunkey Officers' servant or steward.
foo-foo Talcum powder, used to limit perspiration and prickly heat, sometimes violently scented.
fore and aft rig Naval uniform involving peaked cap, jacket, and trousers creased at front and back.
gannet One with a voracious or greedy appetite.
gash Refuse or garbage. This must be disposed of with caution in wartime as it can betray a ship's presence to a submarine, and discarded written material may impart useful information.
Gestapo Regulating Branch personnel.
goofers Idlers and off-duty men who congregate to watch some interesting procedure, sometimes in hazardous circumstances.
green rub Misfortune, an undeserved penalty.
groundbait Small gift, such as stockings or cosmetics, given to female acquaintance, with ulterior motive.
guard and steerage Watchkeepers and other personnel with arduous duties who are allowed extra sleep periods and other privileges.
gulpers A gulp of another's tot of rum, conceded as payment for some service, or as a gambling debt. (See 'sippers'.)
Ghut Notorious street of bars and places of entertainment in Valetta, Malta, riotously frequented by sailors.
Guzz Devonport depot, dockyard and barracks. When affiliated to the Devonport port division, a man is a 'Guzz rating'.
HA High Angle, with particular reference to high-angle anti-aircraft guns.
hard liers Small bonus once paid in compensation for the hard conditions of small ships.
HD Continuous wireless broadcast for warships, 78 K/cs. (See also 'BN'.)

HE High Explosive; also Hydrophone Effect.
heads Latrines, in earlier times always in the head, or bows, of a ship.
herrings-in Tinned herrings in tomato sauce, a frequent breakfast dish.
H/F High Frequency.
HO 'Hostilities Only'; a rating conscripted for the duration of hostilities.
hogwash (hoggin') Sea, sea water.
homers A domestic environment ashore, not necessarily a rating's own home, which he visits. He is then said to be 'up 'omers'.
Hooky Term of address for a leading rating, identified by an anchor badge on his left arm.
Jack Dusty Rating of the Stores Branch; any rating employed in storekeeping.
Jack Strop Belligerent or impertinent rating.
jankers Punishment routine imposed on defaulters.
Jaunty Master-at-Arms, senior rating of naval police branch and probably the most unpopular person in any ship or establishment.
Jimmy, Jimmy the One First Lieutenant, responsible for the smooth running of ship's routine and daily work-programme. (See 'Number One'.)
joss Luck. Bad joss is bad luck, misfortune.
kedge Anchor. To kedge a vessel is to move it by laying out an anchor and then heaving her up to it.
Kil 'Kil'-class patrol sloop, a class with names beginning with 'Kil', e.g., *Kilburnie*, *Kilkenzie*, *Kilmore*, etc.
killick Leading rating of any branch; e.g., killick sparker, killick of the mess, etc.
KR and AI King's Regulations and Admiralty Instructions.
KUA Kit Upkeep Allowance; a small supplement to cover the replacement of uniform kit which, after the first issue, must be purchased by the rating.
kye Cocoa, made from solid bricks of unsweetened chocolate which must be grated or crushed before adding hot water.
lamp swinging Boastful reminiscing.
lamps trimmed Suffer injury or punishment in fight or brawl.
L and PA Lodging and Provision Allowance. Additional payment to ratings who are quartered in private accommodation ashore.
liberty boat Boat (occasionally a road vehicle) taking men ashore for leave.
Lobs! Peculiar to Boys' Service, a shout of warning at the approach of danger, e.g., an officer or instructor.
main brace, splice the To splice the main brace is to issue an extra tot of rum to all hands, usually as a reward following action or a

particularly hard period of work. Originally, the main brace, one of the thickest and heaviest ropes in a ship, was spliced only very occasionally.
make and mend A period of no duties, usually a half-day, originally given to seamen for the purpose of making or mending clothes, but in more recent times for sleeping, shore-going or recreation.
Maltese Lace Ragged or holed clothing, particularly underclothing.
matelot Lower-deck sailor.
messdeck lawyer The equivalent of a barrack-room lawyer; one able to quote chapter and verse of regulations.
mess traps Crockery and utensils used on mess-decks.
Mickey Mouse Motor Mechanic (Naval), from the initials MM.
ML Motor Launch.
M/L Minelayer.
muzzle velocity Tinned meat and vegetables, from the initials M&V.
nap hand Veneral Disease.
Navvy Navigating Officer.
neaters Rum issued undiluted (neat) as opposed to grog, which has water added, and is classified as one-and-one, two-and-one, etc.
Nife lamp Emergency, battery-fed lamp, switched on either manually or automatically when mains electrical supply fails.
NOIC Naval Officer in Charge; the resident naval authority in most seaports.
north-easter Stoppage of pay, from the initials 'NE' in the pay ledger, meaning 'not entitled', and imposing a cold wind of poverty.
nozzer A recently enlisted boy; a raw recruit.
Number One First Lieutenant. (See 'Jimmy the One.')
Number Threes A rating's third-best blue suit. A full kit should include four blue suits, numbered one to four; number fives, white ducks; number six, white drills – through working rigs, overalls, tropical shorts, etc. The 'rig of the day' is specified daily, or for certain duties. Only 'number ones' has gold badges.
nutty Any kind of sweetmeat or confection. The terms 'chocolate', 'toffee', etc., are almost never used.
OA Ordnance Artificer.
OD Ordinary Rating; the lowest rating in men's service.
'Oggie Hot cornish pasty, often eaten ashore or in canteen, particularly in Devonport.
onion A fraction of a knot (nautical measurement of speed). Thus 'ten knots and an onion' would mean something between ten and eleven knots. One knot is a speed of 2,000 yards, a nautical mile, per hour.
OOD Officer of the Day.
OOW Officer of the Watch.
oppo Friend or shore-going companion, from 'opposite number'.

Out pipes Order given to indicate a resumption of work, or shortly before night retirement. Originally meaning that tobacco pipes should be extinguished.
party Any woman, but usually an acquaintance, casual or formal.
Pay Bob Paymaster.
paid off On completion of a commission, possibly of several years, a ship returned to its home port and 'paid off' its company, who returned to depot to await further drafting.
pea doo Pea soup.
pierhead jump Orders to join a ship at extremely short notice.
pigs Officers.
pin-heads Fleet Air Arm personnel, as opposed to ship's company, in aircraft carrier.
Pipe down Order imposing silence, the last routine order of the day, following 'Out pipes'.
P/L Plain language, as opposed to code or cipher.
Pompey Portsmouth depot, dockyard and barracks. Men affiliated to the Portsmouth port division are 'Pompey ratings'.
pom-pom Two-pounder Maxim gun, for both high and low-angle firing.
pongo Soldier.
pusher Woman, usually one of casual acquaintance.
pusser Corruption of 'purser', denoting any item of service issue, whether food, clothing or equipment; the word also describes anything that is correct or conforming to regulations. A 'pusser' ship or person is one that is strict and highly disciplined.
QF Quick Firing.
rabbits Gifts or souvenirs, usually purchased ashore, intended for family or friends at home. A 'rabbit run' is an excursion ashore primarily for the purpose of gift-buying.
rate of knots At high speed. Any journey or activity undertaken speedily is said to be done 'at a rate of knots'.
rattle, in the Faced with disciplinary action.
RDF Radio Direction Finding, by which the bearing of a ship's radio transmission can be determined.
red lead Tinned tomatoes.
red ink A character assessment of 'Excellent', which is written in records in red ink. More normal assessments, in black ink, were 'Very Good', 'Good' or merely 'Satisfactory'.
requestmen Men submitting a request (for leave, advancement, etc.) through official channels. They were interviewed prior to, but on the same occasion as, defaulters.
RNB Royal Naval Barracks.
Roll on my twelve! Frequent *cri de coeur*, referring to the longed-for

expiry of a service engagement, of twelve years or any other period.
Rose Cottage The Veneral Diseases ward in Sick Quarters.
rounds Inspection of ship or establishment by duty officer during late evening; Captain's rounds occurred during Saturday forenoons, following an intensive cleaning programme.
Royals Royal Marines.
R/T Radio Telephony. Voice transmissions, as opposed to morse code (W/T).
rum bosun Rating in mess responsible for collecting and distributing rum issue.
rum rat One with insatiable appetite for rum, both his own and others'.
salt horse An officer of solely seamanship qualifications, as opposed to those with specialist training, e.g., communications, flying, torpedoes, gunnery, etc.
Saturday night sailors Officers and ratings of the Royal Naval Volunteer Reserve.
Sally, The The Salvation Army.
SBA Sick Berth Attendant.
SBNO Senior British Naval Officer.
scran bag All items of kit and clothing left unstowed were confiscated and put into a 'scran bag'. They were subsequently redeemed by their owners on payment of an inch of soap for each item. The soap was used for common cleaning purposes.
scribe Writer; rating of the Navy's clerical branch.
scrub round Ignore, cancel, or take no further action.
SDO Signal Distribution Office.
set A beard, for the growth of which it was necessary to obtain official permission.
shave off To shave off beard, the removal of which must also be officially approved. Also, the expression 'Shave off!' indicates surprise, frustration or disgust.
shite hawks Seagulls, unpopular for their depredation of paintwork and polished brass.
shamfered Damaged. A ship suffering damage in action was said to have been 'shamfered'.
shock To cook. A dish taken to the galley would be accompanied by a request to 'give it a shock'.
short arm inspection Medical Officer's examination of genitals.
sippers A sip of another's rum, conceded as payment for favour or gambling debt. Two sippers equalled one gulpers.
skate Rating with a bad disciplinary record, spending frequent periods under punishment.
slops Items of uniform kit purchased from ship's stores; pusser's issue.

Smoke, The London.
snottie Midshipman, who wears three brass buttons on each cuff, allegedly to prevent them being used to wipe nose.
sparker, Sparks Telegraphist Rating.
Spin a yarn To tell a story in defence of misdemeanour; to deceive by verbosity; boastful reminiscence.
Spithead Pheasant Kipper.
sprog Infant; anyone of immature years.
square rig Naval uniform involving blue jean collar, jumper and bell-bottomed trousers.
squeegee band Improvised musical group utilising mouth organs, combs, clappers, and unusual percussion media.
SRE Sound Reproduction Equipment, for amplifying orders throughout ship, and for radio programmes.
stanchion Rating who has held a comfortable shore posting for unusually long time.
stand easy Brief cessation of work during forenoon and afternoon, usually giving time for a smoke and cup of tea.
station card Small identity card held by all ratings, withdrawn during loss of leave and other privileges.
Stokes Stoker.
stone frigate Any Naval barracks or shore establishment.
Stringbag Swordfish torpedo-carrying biplane.
Stripey Rating with three good-conduct badges (stripes) indicating lengthy service and particularly one who has achieved no promotion. They represent at least thirteen years 'undetected crime'.
stroppy Belligerent, insubordinate. The description of a 'Jack Strop'.
Sub Variously, a sub-lieutenant, a submarine, a loan of money.
swing the lamp To relate or boast of harrowing seafaring experiences, at which a listener might scoff, 'Swing the lamp'.
tailor-made Manufactured cigarette, as opposed to one rolled by hand.
TBS Radiotelephone for 'Talk Between Ships'.
T, G or UA Temperance, Grog, or Under Age. A rating is Under Age until twenty, when he may opt to draw rum (in which case he is defined as 'G') or to draw a small payment in lieu (and so become 'T'). A temperance rating was a *rara avis*.
three-badger See 'Stripey'.
ticket Discharge from the service. To get one's ticket was an enviable achievement.
tickler Cigarette and pipe tobacco allowance, packed in ½lb tins, a duty-free purchase. A hand-rolled cigarette was also a 'tickler'. The name comes from that of a manufacturer of tinned jam.
tiddley Neat, or of good appearance. Applied equally to the tie of a

ribbon, the cut of a suit, or the lines of a ship.
tiffy Artificer, either Engine Room, Ordnance or Electrical.
tiller flat Aftermost compartment of ship, housing emergency steering position and, when applicable, depth-charge stowage.
tinfish Torpedo.
Tombola The Naval equivalent of 'Bingo'.
Torps Torpedo officer or rating.
tot Measure of rum issued to eligible ratings daily, at midday. Rum is denied to defaulters.
Townie Sepcifically, another rating who originates from the same home town, but often used as a friendly form of address.
train smash Tinned tomatoes and bacon.
Uckers A complex version of the table game Ludo, widely played on messdecks.
UJC Union Jack Club; servicemen's hostel near Waterloo Station.
up the line To travel home on leave, as opposed to local leave ashore.
victualled To be officially listed for maintenance by a ship or mess, on permanent or temporary basis, so that accommodation, food and rum can be issued.
VAD Nursing auxiliary of the Voluntary Aid Detachment.
V/S Visual Signalling.
V & W A class of destroyer built between 1917 and 1919, all bearing names beginning with 'V' or 'W', and of which fifty-eight were in service in 1939.
watchkeepers' Extended shore leave and/or sleeping periods allowed to watchkeeping personnel in compensation for long working hours.
Wavy Navy Royal Naval Volunteer Reserve, from the wavy gold bands on the cuff of an RNVR officer which distinguish him from a colleague of the regular Navy.
winger Chosen friend or shore-going companion.
W/T Wireless Telegraphy, generally assumed to mean morse code transmissions as opposed to voice telephony (R/T).

Leslie Thomas
Omerod's Landing 90p

1940: only months after Dunkirk Churchill is determined to set Europe ablaze. Detective-Sergeant George Ormerod of the Metropolitan Police looks like being the first match! Investigating a murder in Wandsworth, he suspects one Albert Smales of the crime; to apprehend him Ormerod travels to the heart of Hitler's Fortress Europe, where Smales – a casualty of Dunkirk – is safely inside a French hospital. With his dog called Formidable and a delectable and ruthless French lady agent, Ormerod makes his landing and finds adventures of more kinds than one!

'Ingenious . . . funny . . . his best book yet' FINANCIAL TIMES

Raymond Carras & William Drummond
Honeycomb 90p

1944: deep under London a trainload of bullion, gems and art treasures travels to a dockland rendezvous *en route* to safety across the Atlantic. Maximum security has failed to hide the plan from the Nazi specialist who sprang Mussolini from the ruins of Fascist Italy – Otto Skorzeny. Skorzeny's scheme – Operation Honeycomb – sends a mercenary strike-force to hijack the treasure train deep underground in a world of rats and slime; a band of men led by Lucas Molyneux, tunnelling engineer by profession, renegade by creed – a man with no flag to call his own . . .

Alexander Fullerton
Patrol to the Golden Horn 85p

The latest thrilling novel in the superb Everard series.

A strike against the battlecruiser *Goeben*, lurking menacingly at Constantinople; an E-class submarine runs the gauntlet of minefields and batteries in the Dardanelles. Aboard E57 is a Marine explosives expert, a taciturn cloak-and-dagger specialist, and Nick Everard, veteran of Jutland and Zeebrugge, taking on a virtual suicide mission . . .

George Fox
Amok 95p

He lives like a wild beast – kills like a professional executioner: they call him the Amok . . .

When the Japanese forces evacuated the Philippines in the last bloody months of the war, one man was left behind – a renegade giant capable of nightmare violence and terrifying brutality, armed with a razor-edged Samurai blade, and ordered to delay the enemy advance as long as possible. Three decades later, he is still killing – a murderous spectre haunting the lives of every man, woman and child in an isolated island community. He's the reason that two men have returned to the Philippines – one has come to kill him, the other to save him.

Wilbur Smith
Hungry as the Sea £1.20

Through shipwreck and hurricane, through the ice-world of the Antarctic and the thundering surf of the African coast, in the arms of the lovely Samantha and on the bridge of his powerful *Warlock*, Berg is a man in his element. Deposed as top man in a huge shipping consortium, he's running a debt-ridden ocean-going salvage outfit – fighting back against the ruthless ambition of the arch-rival who stole his wife and son and robbed him of an empire – hell-bent on retribution . . .

'Surges forward with a bone in its teeth'
TIMES LITERARY SUPPLEMENT

Robert Perrin
Jewels 90p

The night they stole the Irish Crown Jewels – Summer 1907, the eve of Edward VII's visit to Ireland. Two men, both enmeshed in the most dissolute of circles, plan and execute the perfect crime: the theft of the priceless insignia of the Order of St Patrick from the Bedford Tower of Dublin Castle. Captain Richard Gorges: hero of Spion Kop, soldier of fortune, rampant homosexual; Frank Shackleton: Dublin Herald to the Ulster King of Arms, incorrigible con-man and total degenerate . . .